MOONRISE

Danny didn't mean to kill Jerry, fight him. But once Jerry gets a few drinks in him, he has to prove how tough he is. It had always been like that, ever since they were kids. Jerry had always played the bully. When Jerry tells Danny he isn't good enough for Gilly, he lets it go as usual. But when Jerry makes a crack about his father, asking him how it feels to drop six feet at the end of a rope, something just snaps in Danny.

Danny hides the body but he can't hide from himself. He feels everyone's eyes on him, feels the pointing fingers of guilt. Even though Gilly is now going out with him, he can't be himself with her. He will always be the son of a killer—and now a killer himself. Then comes the night when the coon hunt turns up Jerry's corpse, and Danny can't hide from himself any longer.

"*Moonrise* is unique in that it's one of the few noirs in which the redemptive power of love holds nihilism at bay."—Eddie Muller

Theodore Strauss Bibliography
(1912-2009)

Novels:
Night at Hogwallow (Little, Brown, 1937;
    reprinted as *The Haters*, Bantam, 1950)
Moonrise (Viking, 1946; reprinted as *Dark Hunger*, Bantam, 1951)

Selected Filmography

Film:
Moonrise (1948)
Isn't It Romantic? (1948)
The Russian Story (1948)
Four Days in November (1964)

Television:
The Way Out Men (1965)
They've Killed President Lincoln (1971)
The Crucifixion of Jesus (1972)
The Killer Instinct (1973)
Struggle for Survival (1974)
I Will Fight No More Forever (1975)
America Salutes Richard Rodgers: The Sound of His Music (1976)
Jacques Cousteau: Cries from the Deep (1982)
Honeymooners Reunion (1985)
Clue: Movies, Murder & Mystery (1986)

MOONRISE

THEODORE STRAUSS

Introduction by Curtis Evans

Stark House Press • Eureka California

MOONRISE

Published by Stark House Press
1315 H Street
Eureka, CA 95501, USA
griffinskye3@sbcglobal.net
www.starkhousepress.com

MOONRISE
Originally published by The Viking Press, New York, and copyright ©
1946 by Theodore Strauss. Serialized in *Cosmopolitan Magazine*.
Reprinted in paperback by Bantam Books, New York, 1951, as *Dark
Hunger*.

"Glimmers of Light in the Darkness" © 2024 by Curtis Evans

ISBN: 979-8-88601-105-0

Cover & Text design by Mark Shepard, shepgraphics.com
Proofreading by Bill Kelly

First Stark House Press Edition: October 2024

Glimmers of Light in the Darkness

By Curtis Evans

Theodore Herbert Strauss, author of the rural noir crime novel *Moonrise* (1946), grew up mostly in small-town America before making his way, like so many young hopefuls before him, to the crowded, neon lit burgs of, successively, Manhattan and Hollywood. Like the admired film of the same title that was faithfully adapted from it in 1948, Strauss' novel offers a more hopeful vision of man and society than that which one commonly finds in noir, a literary form notorious for its bleak, even nihilistic view of life. Indeed, the film version of *Moonrise* has sometimes been dubbed "anti-noir," a term which could be applied as well to the novel itself. While hardly whitewashing the narrowness and cruelty toward those who were deemed, for whatever parochial reasons, "outsiders" in the smalltown America of the 1930s, where lynchings and other provincial horrors were still taking place yearly, *Moonrise* affords readers glimmers of hope for the possibility of a tortured soul's redemption through transformative acts of humanity. In its sentiments the novel is worlds away from the nasty cynicism of the rural noirist Jim Thompson, for example, and darkly comic novels like *Pop. 1280*. *Moonrise* lets in some light.

The middle of five children of itinerant Mennonite and later Christian Church minister Abraham Frederick Strauss and his wife Helena Krause, both of whom were the children of German immigrants, Theodore Strauss was born December 27, 1912 in Inola, Oklahoma, a tiny community of some four hundred people located about thirty miles directly east from Tulsa. Ted Strauss later estimated that after his birth his family moved more than thirty times around America as his devout father followed his calling of preaching to the masses the redemptive Gospel of Jesus

Christ. By 1920 the Strauss family had left the Midwest for good and relocated to the comparative metropolis of Owego, New York, a town of some seven thousand people on the southern border with Pennsylvania.

Thereafter Ted accompanied his parents and his younger brother and sister in relocating to Crewe, Virginia, a town of some two thousand people located about sixty miles southwest of Richmond that sixty-five years earlier had witnessed some of the last desperate flailing of the decimated Army of Northern Virginia. Crewe surely served the author as the inspiration for both the setting of his first published work of fiction, *Night at Hogwallow*, and for *Moonrise*'s fictional Bradford, Virginia, whose inhabitants—good, bad and something in between—are so convincingly detailed in the novel. Living even briefly in the American South of the Thirties must have made a powerful impression on this young wandering Christian.

For a couple of years after his high school graduation, Ted Strauss labored at a variety of odd jobs, including berry picker, janitor, truck driver and printer's devil. In 1931 at the age of eighteen he moved to the vastly different world of Manhattan, where he found employment at the bottom of the heap in the circulation department of the *New York Times*. Six years later at the tender age of twenty-four he published the pungently titled *Night at Hogwallow*, one of five novellas chosen in a contest for publication by Little, Brown & Co. out of no fewer than 1,340 submitted manuscripts.

The next year the darkly handsome Ted—slim, soulful-eyed and wavy-haired—wed fashionable Manhattan dress designer Mary Catherine Morrison, who previously had been married to novelist and screenwriter Dan Totheroh. Together the couple had a son in 1939. In the 1940s Ted became the *Times*' assistant drama critic under the well-known Bosley Crowther, the influential (if overrated) Roger Ebert of that day; but Ted left his perch at the paper in 1944 to become a screenwriter for Paramount Pictures in California.

Perhaps not coincidentally his wife Mary Catherine successfully sued him for divorce that year, accusing him of cruelty and demanding $460 monthly in alimony (about $8000 a month today), along with custody of their young son, Eric Anton Strauss. Suffering severely from asthma, Mary Catherine Strauss, as she still called herself, in 1945 moved to Tucson, Arizona for her health. When she died there only three years later, Eric was residing in Pasadena with his father and his father's new wife.

The same year that Mary Catherine moved to Tucson, Strauss, now in LA, worked on the script for Paramount's hit technicolor epic *California* (1946), starring Ray Milland and Barbara Stanwyck, and the text of his short second novel, *Moonrise*. In January 1946, before the novel was even published, newspapers announced that Paramount had purchased *Moonrise* from one of its young screenwriters for forthcoming film production. Ted was slated to write the screenplay.

Paramount, however, knocked Strauss out of his catbird seat, selling the film rights to a pair of independent producers who hired William Wellman, director of the recent Academy Award nominated (best picture) rural lynching drama *The Ox-Bow Incident*, along with another screenwriter. Apparently, the lead role of the novel's youthful neurotic killer Danny Hawkins was offered to Jimmy Stewart (!), who sensibly passed on it, leading to Burt Lancaster being considered. In the end John Garfield ended up being slated to play Danny.

After this attempt fell through financially, there was talk of getting John Farrow, director of *California*, with Alan Ladd in the lead. Finally, however, *Moonrise* ended up with low budget studio Republic Pictures, best-known for its popular Roy Rogers westerns. Republic planned the movie as one of its new line of prestige, albeit underfunded, literary pics, alongside *The Red Pony*, based on the John Steinbeck novel, and Orson Welles' rendition of Shakespeare's *Macbeth*. In October 1948 the studio released *Moonrise* to very good reviews but rather poor box office. (For more on the film see below.)

Two years previously *Moonrise* had been serialized in *Cosmopolitan* and published in book form by The Viking Press to strongly positive reviews. The novel was chosen as a selection of the Book League and it eventually reached an impressive total sale of over 300,000 copies. In 1951, Bantam republished *Moonrise* in paperback, along with the long out-of-print *Night at Hogwallow*, respectively retitling the opuses *Dark Hunger* and *The Haters*. Surprisingly, given this success, Theodore Strauss never again published another novel. He had, as they say, other fish to fry in the Fifties.

Ted married twice more, the second time in 1947 to the tragically troubled Dorothy Comingore, a brilliant actress and political leftist who became a victim of pitiless redbaiting and the implacable enmity of powerful newspaper publisher William Randolph Hearst. The mogul had despised the actress' portrayal of his mistress Marion Davies in Orson Welles' classic 1941 film *Citizen Kane* and waged a vendetta campaign against her in Hollywood, employing such venomous proxies as his odious, Commie-coshing gossip columnists Hedda Hopper and Walter Winchell. By this time Ted and Dorothy resided together in Pasadena with Eric and Judith and Michael Collins, Dorothy's daughter and son from her previous marriage to screenwriter Richard Collins. It was just like the Seventies sitcom *The Brady Bunch*, if you threw in, as things terribly transpired, multiple divorces, alcoholism, prostitution and Communism. Facetiousness aside, Michael Collins dubbed it a "Raymond Chandler world."

After only five years of marriage, Ted successfully sued Dorothy, who sadly had developed a serious drinking problem, for divorce at the height of her political troubles in August 1952. A couple of months later she pugnaciously but ill-advisedly testified before the House Un-American Activities Committee (HUAC) in October, refusing to confirm or deny whether she had ever belonged to the Communist Party. Contrarily Richard Collins sang like a canary to HUAC, naming names with abandon, and went on to enjoy a long and lucrative career in showbiz, producing the television series *Bonanza* and *Matlock* and passing away at the age of ninety-eight.

Six years earlier in 1946, at the very inception of his Hollywood career, Ted himself achieved the dubious distinction of being one of the eleven Hollywood screenwriters whom *Hollywood Reporter* publisher William Wilkerson denounced as "avowed Leftists and sympathizers of the [Communist] Party line" in his incendiary HR column "A Vote for Joe Stalin," the first of the many Hollywood blacklists of suspected Communists in the film profession. Most of the Red writers named in the article, which included Dalton Trumbo and Ring Lardner, Jr., indeed were blacklisted, though Ted was not. Doubtless all this harassment placed further stress on Ted and Dorothy's marriage, which was already buckling, according to her son and his stepson Michael Collins, due to their own purely personal conflicts. Their five-year marriage was a "rough relationship," Michael recalled. Dorothy, for example, was displeased when Ted's son Eric came to live with them after his mother became fatally ill.

In 1953 Dorothy's troubles deepened when LA vice cops arrested the actress on a charge of solicitation, which she indignantly claimed was a police set-up in retaliation for her defiant HUAC testimony. Ted successfully petitioned to have his ex-wife committed to the Camarillo State Mental Hospital for chronic alcoholism, in the process obtaining custody of their son Peter, while Richard Collins was awarded custody of his two children with Dorothy, who was forbidden from seeing any of them until they reached the age of twenty-one. (If a film had been made of all this, it might have been titled *Revenge of the Ex-Husbands*.) Released from the psychopathic ward two years later in 1955, Dorothy found herself blacklisted from the entertainment industry, but finally she achieved some measure of happiness in a final marriage, this one to a kindly Connecticut postal worker.

Ted himself was a kind man, according to his stepson Michael, who remembers him as "one of the great guys," a "cosmopolitan" and a "cool guy" who enjoyed his martinis and was someone whom he, Michael, as a young child "really loved." Ted was a keen fisherman, a real western cowboy type, according to Michael, who used to take him along on fishing trips to Idaho every summer as a child. He recalls Ted as a "very handsome," "mild-mannered" and "soft-spoken" man, who only ever became angry with him on one occasion. (He has forgotten what about.) However, when Ted did lose his temper—usually with Dorothy, who, some said, "brought out the worst in men"—his voice took on gravely fearsome tone, sounding rather like the "wrath of God."

With his screenwriting career having petered out (for whatever reasons), Ted found work with *Life* magazine and in 1956 he became editor of the doubtlessly highly patriotic *Woman's Home Companion*. That same year Ted, now forty-four, made his third and final plunge into wedlock with twenty-five-year-old United Airlines stewardess Luann "Ludy" Miller, whom he had met in San Francisco. The third time was the charm. The couple, who had one son together in 1960, remained amicably united in matrimony until Ludy's death a full half-century later in 2006.

From the Sixties through the Eighties Ted achieved distinction as a writer of fictional and documentary films for television. Intriguingly, one of his later documentary films, *Clues: Movies, Murder and Mystery*, deals with mystery fiction and films. (It was narrated by the late Martin Mull and apparently was tied-in with the release of the 1985 cult fan film *Clue*, which co-starred Mull as Colonel Mustard.) Ted received two Emmy nominations for his television scriptwriting, winning one. The first of the film documentaries he scripted, *Four Days in November*, a timely telling of the Kennedy assassination, was nominated for an Academy Award for best documentary in 1965.

During these later years Ted and Ludy travelled the world, often in connection with his film work, and became friends with such famed personalities as oceanographer Jacques Cousteau. Ludy became an early proponent of quilts as serious artwork and in the Eighties and Nineties she owned an antique quilt shop in Santa Monica. Ted passed away three years after his beloved Ludy at Sherman Oaks, California on October 30, 2009 at the age of ninety-six. Of all his artistic accomplishments he remains best known today for having written the novel that served as the basis for the film *Moonrise*.

Moonrise: Novel and Film

Theodore Strauss' *Moonrise* tells the tale of twenty-three-year-old Virginian Daniel Hawkins, orphaned, so-called "hillbilly white trash" from rustic Chinamook up by Black Mountain, whose grandmother sent him to Bradford for his education at the age of ten. Known in Brandon as the boy whose pa was ignominiously hanged for murder—his father went into Bradford and shot to death the lax doctor he blamed for his wife's death—Danny has been cruelly "othered" by many in the town since his arrival thirteen years earlier. His old schoolyard tormenter is Jerry Sykes, a former high school football hero and the sneering, privileged son of the local bigwig, potbellied banker J. B. Sykes. Jerry and Danny are rivals for the affections of the new schoolteacher, lovely, ladylike Gilly Johnson. In the brutal fight in the woods by Brothers Pond which opens the novel, Danny kills Jerry with a rock, rather like Cain slaying Abel in Eden—though Danny and Jerry are only brothers-in-harms, as it were, and Bradford is no Eden. Rather than confess his misdeed, Danny hides Jerry's body down by Brothers Pond. With this fateful act of slaughter committed in the decisive rage of a single deadly moment, Danny falls deep into a pit of his own devising, one which he unrelentingly digs all himself with the dismal spades of his guilt and fear.

In this way Danny only sets himself farther apart from everyone else in the town—even his kindly, pious Aunt Jessie, who took him into her Bradford home and worries over him; even Billy Scripture, the poor deaf and dumb, crippled, sweet natured young man with the simple mind of an innocent young child, of whom Danny, with his instinctive feeling for the victimized, has designated himself a protector; even his black mentor Mose, a former railroad worker like himself who caretakes the crumbling old antebellum mansion at Blackwater Plantation and leads white hunting parties out on "coon hunts"; even Gilly herself, whom Danny loves and who might, just might love him back.

In the view of the novel it is this isolation, this setting apart from humanity, that is the worst possible thing—a point repeated over and over again in the text. "You've always been apart, kind of—like you were afraid of folks or didn't trust 'em," Aunt Jessie tells him. "If you're going to live among people, Daniel, you got to trust them." Thinks Danny bleakly to himself: "There ain't but one person in this whole town that knows who killed Jerry Sykes and that's me," as the realization "came over him that that was the most awful thing of all." Even Mose—better read and smarter than anybody in Bradford, Danny loyally tells Sheriff Clem Otis—suffers from his self-imposed isolation. He tells Danny:

> "Man ought to have a woman, friends anyway. Man ought to live in a world with other folks. Man gets tired of talking to himself, gets tired watching the fireflies and listening to the night and the frogs bellowing in the swamp. When I come out here, I thought I'd be out of the way and nobody would shove me around because of my color. What I did was resign from the human race—and I guess that's about the worst crime there is…. Only they don't hang you for it."

Later on in the novel, as Mose strums "Mr. Guitar," the black man croons a blues song, "Lonesome," which as the lyrics develop contains a pointed message to Danny:

> Daylight coming in the morning,
> Hangman waiting on the stones,
> Rope hanging from the gallows,
> Pit waiting for my bones,
>   Lonesome.
>
> Don't send me flowers,
> Don't send me mail,
> And where I'm going,
> I won't need bail,
>   Lonesome.

Can Danny rejoin society after breaking the weightiest of its

Christian God's stern commandments? Is there any way back to people after what he has done? Or like a Cornell Woolrich antihero is he condemned forever to a miserable, lonesome life of isolation, incubated by his guilt and fear? Will Sheriff Clem Otis manage to bring Jerry's death home to Danny, even if the introspective lawman does not seem at all the keenest hunter in the pack? ("You should have been a preacher, Clem, not a bloodhound," the coroner mockingly tells him.) Yet even were Danny to evade the hard hand of justice, could he ever get relief from the incessantly pricking fingers of his own conscience?

Unsurprisingly some reviewers deemed *Moonrise* a Dixie Dostoevsky, a sort of hillbilly *Crime and Punishment*, if you will; yet this observation was not made in order to diminish the novel as mere imitation, plebian paste to Dostoevsky's authentic diamond. To the contrary, reviews of the novel were largely positive, praising not only the sheer thrills of its crime narrative but also the moving sincerity and moral force of its humane, democratic vision. "*Moonrise* is in part a psychological novel about a miserable backcountry youth who never had a chance…. It is also an exciting story of violent murder and … almost unendurable suspense," wrote a Canadian reviewer in *The Province*, who additionally pronounced *Moonrise* "an excellent book, done with macabre skill." Declared Sam Ragan, editor of the Raleigh *News and Observer*: "This is not a new story … but it is remarkably well told. Once you have started reading it, you will find it hard to stop until you have finished." Echoed Kelsey Guilfoil, books editor of the *Chicago Tribune*: "About the only thing wrong with this novel is that there isn't enough of it…. It's the sort of story you read at one sitting, not only because of its brevity, but because it grips you and flows in such a smooth narrative stream … Strauss' prose is hard and lean; his effects are simply managed and achieved with a deceptive ease that must have cost him much labor."

Stauss' treatment of the character of Mose deserves some special mention for the black man is arguably the moral center of the novel (or perhaps he shares this space as well with Clem Otis). The author's first novel—which concerns a black man menaced by a lynch mob in a southern state—was published in 1937, not long after an anti-lynching bill was defeated in Congress due to obstruction from Southern politicians determined to preserve what they themselves proudly termed "white supremacy." By making the outcast Danny's best friend and moral preceptor an eloquent black man who self-isolated to insulate himself from the raging contagion of the white man's racism, Strauss again condemns, if more implicitly this time, racial injustice. Significantly, in citing *Night at Hogwallow* in a 1939 academic article, "The American Race Problem as Reflected in American Literature," black scholar Sterling A. Brown passingly referred to Strauss as a "leftwing" writer.

This ideological concern, leftwing or not, with American racial injustice was one which Strauss shared with his second wife, Dorothy Comingore, who today is celebrated, at least in liberal corners, as a brave, outspoken martyr of McCarthyism and rampant anticommunist hysteria. Among behavior that redbaiting congressmen deemed suspicious was Dorothy's staunch support for black civil rights. For her part, Strauss' third wife Ludy on the eve of her death in 2006 was preparing displays of her collection of African-American quilts.

If there is a fly in *Moonrise*'s ointment, it is perhaps the novel's attitude to women. While Gilly is portrayed as a blonde saint and Jessie's aunt and grandmother are sympathetic righteous country matrons, the novel otherwise offers readers a parade of pecking harpies, from Jimmy Biff's flirtatious, giggly girlfriend Julie, who "liked to neck with just about anybody," to the tourist trade harridan at the roadhouse who cruelly toys with Billy Scripture and the backbiting women of the Ladies Aid Society, the worst of whom is Martha Otis, wife of the sheriff. In a passage that takes place at home with Martha, where she upbraids her husband for, as she sees it, mishandling the investigation into Jerry Sykes' murder, it is clear that Clem deems his wife a sadly untamed shrew. "Why did women's voices become so unpleasant after forty," he wonders dismally. The worst moment for Clem is when his wife tucks in to sleep beside him: "By the time he'd gotten into his nightshirt and climbed into bed, Martha had come out of the bathroom. Clem took one look at her and turned away." He thinks to himself: "When she's young woman shows her best side to her husband. But when she's older she shows her best side to strangers."

Perhaps Clem's reflections help explain Ted Strauss' pair of short-lived, acrimonious marriages. More problematic yet is when wise man Mose tells Danny of the poor boxcar bum whom he once took mercy upon who later was jailed "for trying to make love to a girl who turned out to be the constable's daughter." Asks Mose rhetorically: "Guilty? That's what Mr. Law wrote on the books. But guilty of what? Guilty of wanting a little loving. They give him fifteen years for being lonesome...." The modern reader might want a little more detail about the bum and this constable's daughter before they agree with Mose on this one.

Still, this is but a comparatively minor blemish on a superb popular psychological crime novel (noir or anti-noir, take it as you will), one that strangely to me was allowed to fall out of print for decades after 1951, despite the fact that Strauss himself only died fifteen years ago. That *Moonrise* is remembered at all today is due to its wondrous, lightning-in-a-bottle translation into the film of the same name, which upon its reissue as a Criterion Collection DVD in 2018 was hailed by many bloggers as something of a masterpiece.

■ ■ ■

Although Republic Pictures sometimes is dismissed as a "Poverty Row" studio, the company managed to put together a fantastic production team and cast for *Moonrise*. The film was helmed by acclaimed, two-time Oscar winning director Frank Borzage—one of the acknowledged greats of silent film and early talkies who in the Forties had been a bit on his uppers creatively—and shot by John L. Russell, cinematographer of Orson Welles' *Macbeth* and Alfred Hitchcock's *Psycho*. (Welles once proclaimed him the best man in his field.) The art direction was done by seven-time Oscar nominee Lionel Banks (his last film; he died two years later at the age of forty-eight), who worked miracles on a small budget, designing a convincing southern town and country setting, complete with a dance hall and carnival, while markedly whittling the cost of construction from $125,000 down to $28,000. The *LA Times* reported of Banks' cost-cutting marvels:

> Banks' settings are realistic and, more important, economical. On one stage 120x200 feet, he has constructed a Virginia swamp, which also doubles for a lake and a lagoon. The same stage has an old southern mansion, a sleepy little town and a resort complete with a Ferris wheel.
>
> The swamp later will become a forest. A hidden cabin occupies one part of this amazing set, where Dane Clark will find refuge following a wild flight through the swampland.... On Stage No. 4, instead of using an expensive railroad set a train's arrival will be simulated by a shadow moving across the station (really just a front) and steam blown across the scene.

These settings are amazingly effective in tandem with the film's astonishing black and white cinematography, some of the most evocative work ever done in a noir film. *Moonrise* justifiably could have snagged across-the-board Oscar nominations, in my view, but in the event the film achieved but a single nod, for sound. The cast hired to play the parts in the film was similarly impressive.

In the lead as Danny Hawkins was thirty-five-year-old Dane Clark. Often dubbed the "poor man's John Garfield," Clark—whose Jewishness was, like Garfield's, concealed behind a WASPish stage name (his real one was the uneuphonic Bernard Elliot Zanville)— was a compelling actor in his own right who never really made the big time. He graduated from Cornell University and St. John's Law School in Brooklyn before turning to acting on the stage. Like others before him he went from stage to film in Hollywood, but he did not achieve credited roles until 1943, when he was thirty-one years old. Probably his best-known film is the Bette Davis identical twins melodrama, *A Stolen Life* (1946), where he had a major supporting part, but his best turn before *Moonrise* (1947) was as the male lead in Jean Negulesco's *Deep Valley*, which told the story of a chain-gang fugitive who falls in love with the shy farmgirl who shelters him, played by Ida Lupino (sometimes dubbed the "poor man's Bette Davis"). Oddly enough the film was adapted from a novel by Dan Totheroh, meaning that Dane Clark starred successively in films adapted respectively from novels by Mary Catherine Morrison's first and second husbands.

Dane Clark's tough guy intensity, reminiscent of Jimmy Cagney, lent itself to crime films and he effectively played supporting villains in such films as *Without Honor* (1949) and *Backfire* (1950); yet it was overseas in the Fifties that he achieved his finest leading movie roles, in a series of crime and noir films: *Le Traque / Gunman in the Streets* (1950, France, co-starring Simone Signoret); *Highly Dangerous* (1951, England, co-starring Margaret Lockwood and directed by Roy Ward Baker with a screenplay by Eric Ambler based on his novel *The Dark Frontier*); *The Gambler and the Lady* (1952, England, Hammer Films); *Blackout* (1954, England, Hammer Films, directed by Terence Fisher, based on a Helen Nielsen crime novel); and *Paid to Kill* (1954, England, Hammer Films). He became a staple on American television for over three decades, appearing, naturally enough, on many cop and crime shows. His last acting job was on a 1989 episode of *Murder, She Wrote*.

Although few initially would imagine Dane Clark as a racoon hunting backwoods southern boy (he is also a bit too old for the part, as were John Garfield and Alan Ladd, not to mention Burt Lancaster and Jimmy Stewart), Clark portrays his anguished, neurotic character with both wounding intensity and wounded sensitivity. Matching him are female lead Gail Russell as the angelic schoolteacher Gilly Johnson, who is so positively luminous in the role that you will readily forget Gilly is supposed to be a blonde. Russell also memorably played similarly sweet, lovely characters entrapped in frightening situations in the genre films *The Uninvited*, 1944, *The Unseen*, 1945, and *Night Has a Thousand Eyes*, 1948.

Outstanding in the major supporting parts are Allyn Joslyn, typically a specialist in drolly depicting "pompous, wealthy snobs," effectively cast against type as Danny's gently philosophizing, introspective lawman nemesis, Clem Otis; a wise though melancholy Rex Ingram as Mose, whose haunting rendition of "Lonesome" is one if the film's high points; a memorably poignant Harry Morgan of *M*A*S*H* fame as Billy Scripture (surely worthy of an Oscar nomination); and third-billed Ethel Barrymore in her brief appearance as Danny's stately mountaineer grandmother. The smaller parts, all drawn from the novel, are uniformly finely played, with handsome crooner David Street as slick band leader Ken Williams, who falls under the sheriff's suspicion for the murder; Selena Royle as kindly but uncomprehending Aunt Jesse; Irving Bacon as comically forgetful hardware merchant Judd Jenkins, who maddeningly keeps mentioning that hunting knife Danny lost; Phil Brown, best known for playing Luke Skywalker's uncle in *Star Wars*, as incessantly slangy soda jerk Elmer; vulturous Charles Lane as the mysterious and menacing Man in Black; a heavily made-up Houseley Stevenson, the creepy plastic surgeon from Humphrey Bogart's *Dark Passage* (1947), as wizened Uncle Joe Jingle, once a bugle boy at Appomattox, who still cannot abide Yankees; and a blondly bullying and arrogant Lloyd Bridges as doomed Jerry Sykes. Even uncredited roles have striking authenticity, like John Harmon's seedy baseball toss game attendant and Archie Twitchell's relentlessly pattering barker at the belly dancer peep show. ("The county fair—your own county fair—presents for the first time the Syrian enchantresses direct from the forests of Lebanon!...Hurry, hurry, hurry!")

Tasked with scripting was Charles F. Haas (his sole writing credit), who also produced the film. His screenplay is singularly faithful to the novel, drawing the great majority of its dialogue and scenes straight from the text. Some intelligent alterations are made for the movie, most notably the great opening montage showing the hanging of Danny's father (in shadows) and the early schoolyard taunting that Danny endured, reminiscent of the infamous jingle about Lizzie Borden's forty whacks. ("Danny Hawkins' dad was hanged! Danny Hawkins' dad was hanged!"). Additionally, the film excised book passages set at the lowly roadhouse, at a gossipy

Ladies Aid Society meeting at Aunt Jessie's, and at the home of the unhappily yoked Clem and Martha Otis—all of which serves effectively to tighten the narrative focus on Danny. All in all, it is a masterful testament both to Haas' scripting and the leanness of Strauss' writing. Rarely has a novel been so well and faithfully served by a film script.

With the exception of the opening montage, the film's fine set pieces are almost entirely derived from the novel, like the fatal fight by Brothers Pond; Danny's manic car drive and wreck with his terrified passengers; his endurance of a well-meant inquisition from Aunt Jessie as he symbolically stands beside a looming fishbowl; the raccoon hunt where Danny angrily shakes the trapped "coon" from a tree branch, then bursts into a fit of weeping as the pack of blood lusting hound dogs violently dispatch it; Billy Scripture trying futilely to fit his feet to those long-ago youthful footprints he made in a cement sidewalk; Danny's frantic near-fatal assault on Billy to recover his lost hunting knife, which he dropped at the scene of the crime; and the intensely claustrophobic Ferris wheel scene at the county fair. There are a few intelligent tweaks here and there, to be sure, like having Danny and Gilly charmingly waltz together at the decayed antebellum mansion at Blackwater Plantation; putting the sheriff and his bluenose wife on the Ferris wheel with Danny and Gilly; and giving youthful soda jerk Elmer an amusing penchant for Forties hepster lingo.

Yet the film stays true to the message of the book, frequently even enhancing it with filmic technique in its superb editing and cinematography, which relies heavily on striking transitions and visuals that could have appeared in the heyday of silent film. In his review of *Moonrise*, Theodore Strauss' former colleague at the *New York Times*, Bosley Crowther, pronounced that while the acting in the film was strong, "the book towers above the picture" because the visual medium was unable to give full body to the book's characters. I would argue, however, that the film impressively complements the book. Despite his distaste for the squalid, macabre aspect to *Moonrise*—tellingly he had condemned Monogram's violent hit 1945 gangster movie *Dillinger*, which he deemed crudely exploitive—the film's idealistic and romantic director Frank Borzage obviously responded to the novel's humanitarian vision.

One praiseful reviewer stated that *Moonrise* proved that even in the darkly cynical era of Forties noir "Borzage ... still knows his way around with a megaphone." Indeed, as Eddie Muller put it in *Dark City: The Lost World of Film Noir*:

> If ever there were proof that film noir "infected" Hollywood—like a virus of resurgent creativity—it was Borzage's *Moonrise*.... Because crime dramas relied on hypercharged emotions, an old warhorse like Borzage was able to indulge his flair for pictorial storytelling, not restrain it. Like the best of the silents, *Moonrise* drew emotion directly from its juxtaposition of images.

Readers of *Moonrise* should see the film and viewers of *Moonrise* should read the novel. Both media offer crime drama fans memorable noir (or anti-noir?) experiences.

—July 2024
Memphis, Tennessee

....

Curtis Evans received a PhD in American history in 1998. He is the author of *Masters of the "Humdrum" Mystery: Cecil John Charles Street, Freeman Wills Crofts, Alfred Walter Stewart and British Detective Fiction, 1920-1961* (2012), *Clues and Corpses: The Detective Fiction and Mystery Criticism of Todd Downing* (2013), *The Spectrum of English Murder: The Detective Fiction of Henry Lancelot Aubrey-Fletcher and G. D. H. and Margaret Cole* (2015) and editor of the Edgar nominated *Murder in the Closet: Essays on Queer Clues in Crime Fiction Before Stonewall* (2017). He writes about vintage crime fiction at his blog The Passing Tramp and at Crimereads.

MOONRISE

• •

THEODORE STRAUSS

For Harry and Ernest

Chapter One

Danny had never seen a face so speechless and yet so full of an agony to cry out. It lay back now in the tall grass at the water's edge, the neck strained as if in an effort to avoid a blow, the mouth wide open and pulled down to one side like a man trying to scream in a nightmare, trying to scream and having no sound come out. One arm was circled above the head, the hand still squeezing a little clump of grass and root. The rest of him was stretched out like the farmer and his wife that Danny had seen once beside the track at Millers Crossing—loose and twisted as if their bones had suddenly dissolved in them. Jerry could almost be asleep and dreaming. Only he wasn't asleep, and dead men don't have dreams.

He hadn't meant to kill Jerry Sykes, hadn't even meant to fight him. Trouble was Jerry had never learned when to lay off or to keep his mouth shut after he'd had a couple of drinks. It was as if he had to prove to himself what a tough guy he really was by pushing other guys around, especially the ones that weren't liable to kick back. Well, Danny hadn't kicked back when Jerry had told him to stick to the girls at Roy's saloon, that Gilly Johnson was out of his class. He'd kept quiet even when Jerry told him that no ordinary girl from town would go out with him because they were afraid of him. But when Jerry asked if Danny's father had ever told him how it felt to drop six feet at the end of a rope, even Jerry knew that for once he'd said too much.

They were standing between a couple of cars outside the dance at the time and Danny told him to be down on the path beside the pond in five minutes. And that was how it started—just a plain ordinary fight with the fists and then closing in until they weren't just hitting anymore, but they were grappling, trying to get hold, trying to hurt bad. At first Jerry thought he was winning and he kept boring in, trying to throw in the hit that would put Danny on the ground. But Danny wouldn't take the fall. He'd dodge or sidestep and cut Jerry across the face or belly with the kind of short hard blow that doesn't count for much by itself but adds up after a while like nickels in a bank. Jerry was heavier by thirty pounds and he had more reach but he was softer than he was willing to admit. Danny knew that if he waited long enough, Jerry would tire himself out, that he'd loosen up and leave himself wide open.

The funny thing was that Jerry was getting more tired every time he threw his fist, but every time Danny hit Jerry he felt stronger—stronger, because every time his fist smacked into Jerry's soft middle or smashed Jerry's mouth against his teeth Danny knew he was paying back. He was paying back for that first day at grade school when he was the new kid and Jerry had whipped him with the whole playground backing him. He was paying back for the night Jerry and his gang took him into the alley and tarred him because Jerry said he'd squealed to the principal. He was paying back for the scar on his shoulders left by Jerry's cleats in scrimmage seven years ago. He was paying back for every dirty crack Jerry had ever made about him or his father in public or private, to his face and behind his back. Paying back. Paying back good.

Jerry must have caught wise to what Danny was after, must have known that he had to finish the fight in a hurry or Danny would whip him. He got desperate and, just as Danny had figured, Jerry began to hit wild. He made one last rush, and Danny met it with a left hook that made Jerry's eyes close tight and brought a grunt of pain out of him. After that Danny began pushing, ramming in close, jolting his fists quick and short under Jerry's ribs, driving him back, always back. He wasn't paying any attention to Jerry's slow fists anymore. He just kept wedging in and hitting and it was almost a surprise when suddenly Jerry stumbled and went down.

For a minute Danny stood back catching his breath, not knowing whether Jerry was going to get up or not. He saw Jerry half raise himself, heard Jerry's voice hoarse and far away, "You think you've whipped me. Not yet you haven't." Danny didn't answer. He just looked at Jerry's battered face and knew he hated that face, that he'd always hated it and didn't know how much till just that minute.

He knew that he had Jerry beat and cornered, that Jerry was fighting him alone and no playground full of kids to back him up, and that when Jerry got to his feet again it wouldn't be for long.

He waited while Jerry stood up and began moving toward him. It wasn't till he came close that Danny knew Jerry had something in his hand. When Jerry lifted his arm, Danny dodged, felt the rock strike his shoulder and a quick pain jerk through it. The next minute he had wrenched Jerry's arm back, the hand opened and the rock belonged to Danny. He saw Jerry back away and followed him. A hate like lightning stabbed through Danny and at last he leaped. For just a second he felt Jerry's arms close around his waist as he fell and then Danny brought his own arm down with all the strength in him. He felt something crush under his hand and wondered how it was that a man's fist could do all that and then Jerry was lying in the grass not trying to catch his breath anymore. Somewhere under the dark, matted hair the blood began oozing slowly out, a bright thread of it moving around in front of the left ear, across the neck, and into the ground.

Danny must have blacked out after that because he didn't remember a thing until he heard a splash and it took him a minute to place it—somebody had gone off the diving board at Brothers Landing. He looked across the pond and saw an arm flash white out of the water, and behind the diving board he could see the lights of the dance hall on the second floor of the boat house. The Seven Serenaders were playing "Put Your Arms around Me, Honey—Hold Me Tight," and it came to him of a sudden that they'd been dragging it out like this for the past fifteen minutes and he hadn't heard it. Now it sounded like music from another world. It wasn't much more than fifteen minutes ago that he was minding his own business. And Jerry—Jerry was dancing with Gilly, dancing like there was nobody else on the floor.

Well, Jerry was through now with dancing, through with being Sir Galahad in a red Buick, through with making dirty cracks about people he didn't figure were as good as he was. He wouldn't go rushing around the country in that shiny roadster anymore, scaring chickens. He wouldn't come into Billy's Drug anymore wearing a sweater with a "B" as big as his chest because once, by gosh, he was the best fullback that ever played for Bradford High. He wouldn't bother Billy Scripture anymore by teasing him and taking junk away from him just because Billy couldn't hear and couldn't talk and wasn't any brighter than he ought to be. Jerry wasn't even going to be president of his old man's bank and live in the biggest house in town. Jerry was dead at Brothers Pond and his face was covered with mud and blood.

Danny looked down at the dead man for a minute before he heard another sound, like somebody coming down the path. The voices came closer, talking and laughing. He recognized Bill Edmonds' voice, but not the girl's—Edmonds was on the make and he was doing most of the talking. Danny didn't even listen to what he said exactly. He was wondering if Edmonds was going to notice anything, the bushes trampled or branches cracked. He was even afraid they might hear his heart beating. But they went on past, not five yards from where Danny was sitting. He could see the girl's white skirt waving against the bushes.

He got up and began to pull his clothes into shape and try to figure what to do with Jerry. He thought Edmonds and the girl would follow the path till it hit the swamp, and come back. That gave him not more than fifteen minutes, maybe less, and he had to work fast. There were some trees and brake hanging over the edge of the pond and he dragged Jerry's body down under the branches. He put a couple of rocks in his pockets—not enough, but all he had time to find—and left him there, face up. Afterward he closed the bushes around the body as best he could and returned to where they'd done most of the fighting. He couldn't find anything lying around, so he went to the edge of the pond and washed his face and hands and combed his hair. He sat down for a few more minutes so that his face wouldn't look too flushed. Then he buttoned his coat to hide the rip in his shirt and went back to the dance.

Right away he saw Jimmy Biff prowling around the cars parked outside the dance hall. He could hear talking in the back seats and some of the kids were drinking. Nobody noticed him—only Jimmy.

Danny asked, "Where's your girl?"

"That's what I'm trying to find out," said Jimmy. "Last I see she come out here with Bill Edmonds and that was near half an hour ago. I'm going to give her a piece of my mind she won't forget."

"You tell her, Jimmy."

"Hey, where you going? I'm going to blow in about five minutes."

"I'll be right back," Danny said. "I'm going in to the dance and see what's around."

"Ain't nothing," said Jimmy, pretty sour. "What's good is all taken."

"Maybe I'll take it anyway."

Jimmy came around from the back of one of the cars. "Who?" he asked.

"Wait and see."

"Not Annabelle?"

"No. Not Annabelle."

Jimmy shrugged his shoulders as if it didn't much matter. "Don't forget," he said. "Five minutes. If you ain't here by then I'm going to take the car back all by myself and the heck with it."

"I won't forget." Danny stretched out his hand. "Give me a drink."

Jimmy hesitated before he pulled the bottle out of his pocket and handed it to Danny. He watched the whisky go down. "Jeez," he said, "don't take it all."

Danny gave the bottle back to Jimmy and went toward the stairs leading up to the second floor where the dance was. The stairs seemed crowded with people, young kids mostly—girls with hair loose and falling around their shoulders, and guys, their hair slick and eyes excited, with their arms around the girls. Danny looked at them as if they were in a dream, listening to the music and thinking it wasn't real, that all the kids looked familiar but if he were to try and touch them they'd run away. One of the girls saw Danny staring at her and turned her shoulder suddenly away from him. He wanted to hit her for that, but instead he just grinned and went up the stairs.

It was crowded and the men in the band were blowing and sweating. Danny felt hot and a little dizzy, so he lit a cigarette and stood there exhaling the smoke and watching the dancers slide by slowly on the packed floor. He couldn't find what he was looking for, and for a minute he thought she might have gone out and he got a sudden sick feeling as if that slug from Jimmy's bottle had kicked him in the middle, but hard. Then she passed him, dancing very quiet among the others, her hand on her partner's shoulder— Saul Anderson, the football coach. He saw her eyes, wide open and gray-blue—the look that had stopped him the first time he'd seen her—and then the back of her swung around. Nice shoulders, nice waist, nice hips, nice legs. All nice.

But it was the eyes that troubled him most—the startled eyes he had first seen in the beam of his flashlight on the coon hunt a year before. Mose had said there was a new schoolteacher in the crowd, but Danny hadn't thought anything of it until he was standing alone at the edge of the swamp, listening for the dogs, and a hand suddenly brushed his sleeve in the darkness. "What are they stopping for?" a woman's voice had asked. Her hand rested familiarly in his before Danny spoke, "You've got the wrong party, lady." He switched on his flashlight, saw her eyes widen in surprise. "Oh, I thought—" she stopped. "Who are you?" she had asked abruptly. "Daniel Hawkins," he answered. "I help handle the dogs." "Oh. My name's Gilly—Gilly Johnson." Beyond them there was a rashing in the brush and a man's voice had called out her name. Danny had held the light steady for another moment while he said, "Your friend's looking for you." He flicked the light off and she was gone. Danny often remembered that first meeting. And when they sometimes passed on Main Street or saw each other across a dance floor, Danny wondered whether Gilly didn't sometimes remember that meeting too.

The music was getting louder. Danny stepped on his cigarette and went across the floor. He put his hand on Anderson's shoulder. "Excuse me." he said. "I'm cutting in." That same startled look came into Gilly's eyes as she looked from Danny's face to Anderson's, but Anderson looked at Danny as if he were drunk. "Are you kidding?" he asked.

"I'm not kidding," Danny said. "This is my dance."

Anderson moved back a step and Danny moved in. Gilly shrugged her shoulders at Anderson as if she didn't want any trouble and then Danny swung her around and her eyes were looking right into his.

"You're not very courteous," she said, and added, "Not so close, Daniel."

Danny didn't pay any attention and he didn't talk. He didn't know what to talk. All he knew was that he had his arm around Gilly Johnson and it was good and he wasn't going to let go, not to anybody. But he could see that Gilly was thinking of ways to get rid of him without a big fuss there among the high school kids.

"Daniel, I think I'll sit out the rest of this dance," she said once. He didn't answer—just swung her around in a circle till they were both dizzy. And Gilly said, "What's come over you?"

Danny grinned down at her and said, close to her ear, "You ain't dancing with anybody else tonight, Gilly."

She braced an arm against him so she could pull back her head and shoulders and he could see her eyes fighting him. Then she shrugged her shoulders again and they went on dancing.

"I got a car outside," Danny said. "Jimmy Buff's waiting for me with his old man's car. You come with us."

"Certainly not." Danny could tell by the way her lip tightened that Gilly was getting angry.

"Then I'll carry you out," he said.

"You'll—" she started to say, but she saw he meant it. She dropped her arm and walked straight across the floor and down the stairs with Danny following her.

When Jimmy saw what Danny had brought down from the dance he sucked in his breath and said, "Holy gee!" He turned to Gilly, pretty embarrassed. "Howdy-do, Miss Johnson."

Gilly smiled back at him, almost as if he'd just raised his hand in the classroom, almost as if all this didn't mean anything. "You boys going to drive me home?" she asked.

"I guess that's right," said Jimmy. He didn't sound very happy about it.

Danny held open the door while Gilly got into the front seat. Then he turned back toward Jimmy. "Where's Julie?" he asked.

"I found her," said Jimmy. "I give her two minutes."

"She wasn't kissing Bill Edmonds by any chance?"

Jimmy didn't want to talk about it. "Never mind," he said.

Danny pushed him next to the car. "Listen, Jimmy," he told him. "I'm going to drive back—see?"

"Aw, for gosh sake," Jimmy said. "If anything happens to the car my old man will kill me."

"Nothing's going to happen," Danny said. "Only I'm going to take Gilly home alone in it. I'll drop you and Julie at Billy's Drug when we get to town. I'll come back for you later."

Jimmy didn't like the setup a bit. "Jeez, Dan," he whispered, "you're looking for trouble. She's a schoolteacher. Besides, what am I going to do with Julie in a drugstore?"

"Buy her a soda."

Jimmy kicked the tire with his foot but shut up. A minute later Julie came around the car giggling and with all her lipstick off. She looked at Jimmy's face and quickly jumped into the back seat before she saw who was sitting in front. "Where we going, kids?" she asked, happy.

Gilly answered, "Home, I think."

"Oh, Miss Johnson!" Danny could almost hear Julie's jaw drop. When Jimmy climbed into the back seat she gave him a dig and made a question mark with her shoulders. But Jimmy was so mad he would hardly look at her. "I wasn't doing anything," Danny heard Julie say as he started the engine.

He was slipping the gear into reverse when Jimmy said, "You can't back out this way. You're blocked." Danny turned to look out the window and for the first time he noticed the big red roadster right in back of Jimmy's sedan.

"That's Jerry Sykes's car," said Jimmy. "He's got to move it before you can get out."

"I can make it," Danny said very quick. He started to blow the horn at a couple of kids necking in the car ahead.

"Just a minute," said Jimmy. "I'll go up and bring Jerry down here. He's in the dance."

"Never mind," Danny said. He put his hand on the horn again and kept it there till the kids up ahead got the idea. A minute later their car rolled forward and Danny opened up the sedan with a jerk and wheeled out behind them, fast. Jimmy was still beefing when they turned out of the parking yard. "What's the hurry?" he said to Danny. "You nearly clipped the fender just then."

Danny turned in the front seat so sudden that Jimmy thought he was going to hit him. "I'm driving," Danny said between his teeth. "You shut your goddamn mouth!"

They drove up the lane to the macadam highway and turned left toward town. It was Saturday night but it was late and there wasn't too much traffic on the road, so Danny let the engine hum. Every now and then he'd bear down on the accelerator and watch the little needle on the dashboard go up to sixty, sixty-five, seventy— but Jimmy would start getting nervous and Danny would let up on it. It gave Danny a feeling he'd never had before, pushing down like that and letting her ride and watching the fence posts stand up white and disappear alongside in the dark like comets or rockets or something. It was like running away from the world. Or maybe it was something entirely different, like running smack into it. Just the whiz of the tires on the curves and maybe a pair of headlights bearing down on them, and then moving through the dark again. Moving—moving like hell on wheels.

The night was pitch black and the wind whipped through the window, cold and wet, like there was a storm coming up. It was quiet too. Strange, he'd almost forgotten that Gilly was sitting there next to him or that Jimmy and his girl were in the back. He didn't know whether the kids were so quiet because they were scared or whether they were just necking. He guessed they were necking— Julie liked to neck with practically anybody. But in the seat beside him, Gilly was quiet too, and looking straight ahead. He didn't know what was going on in her mind.

"What you thinking about?" he asked.

Gilly half came out of her thoughts and smiled a little—the first time. "I don't know," she said. "What were you thinking about?"

"That'll cost you a buck," he said.

She shrugged her shoulders and didn't answer. After a minute

Danny said, "That was a lie you told me just now. You were thinking about something and you knew what it was. Secret?"

"Not particularly."

"What was it?"

"I was just thinking that you should be a little more like Jerry Sykes."

He wasn't expecting that one. He gripped the steering wheel a little tighter. "Yeah? What's so special about Jerry Sykes?"

"He has good manners. He asks a lady if she'll dance."

"Buy you a drink," he said.

He swung off the highway into the cindered yard of the roadhouse that Roy had changed over from an old broken-down farm building. The neon sign on the front had been turned off and the screen porch was dark, but he could hear the jukebox going inside.

Gilly got out of the car, straightening her dress. "I don't know whether I want to go in there," she said.

"It ain't the country club," Danny said, "but the company's better. Come on, you kids," he called into the back, "refreshments."

He saw their two white faces close together in the dark. "Listen, Dan," Jimmy said, "I don't want you to get all tanked up and then figure on driving."

"What's worrying you?"

"The old man, if you want to know. Jeez creepers, if he knew—"

"Come on. I ain't put a scratch on her."

"I don't want any to get there either," said Jimmy.

"Don't worry, Jimmy," said Gilly. "We'll all have just one drink and then Daniel can drive us home."

Julie gave Jimmy a shove out of the car. "Jimmy, stop fussing," she said. "Daniel isn't a bit drunk."

Jimmy got out of the car but he gave Danny a queer look. "No?" he asked.

It was dim inside as usual and not many folks around—just a table of drunks near one end of the bar and a few farmhands dancing around as mournful as gravediggers with some of the local talent. A couple of men were hanging over the bar talking to Roy and drinking, but they stopped talking when the girls came in.

One of the farmers said uh-uh because Gilly was looking smoky in that dress she was wearing and Julie looked pretty too, but a kid. Gilly and the young ones sat down at a table in the corner away from the jukebox while Danny walked over to the bar. Roy put down his cigarette with the tip sticking over the edge and came toward Danny. "We don't cater to angels in this joint," he said. "Who's the dame?"

"Friend of mine."

Roy shrugged his shoulders. "I said who's the dame—but who cares? What'll you have?"

"Three bourbons and water, and one corn this high—" Danny held four fingers against a glass.

At that moment he felt a hand pull at his sleeve and turned. A blond boy was standing there, smiling and bobbing his head with a sort of baby eagerness. But even when he smiled the boy had a sad, ageless kind of face that could have been thirteen or thirty, and the bright blue eyes had a look in them as if they were always trying to figure something but couldn't quite make it.

"Hello, Billy," Danny said. Folks always talked out loud to Billy Scripture even if they knew that Billy hadn't been able to hear or talk since he was born.

Billy brushed his hand across Danny's sleeve a couple of times, almost as if he were petting him—the only way Billy had of showing people he was friendly. Then he held out his hand. Danny shrugged his shoulders to tell Billy that he didn't know what he wanted.

"He wants a nickel," said Roy. "For the jukebox. You'd think he could enjoy the music the way he's been standing in front of it for the last hour and a half. I guess he gets a boot out of watching the insides change records." Roy set a bottle of bourbon on the bar. "An hour and a half and me with a splitting headache. But it's better than having to watch my bar spoons."

"Here." Danny took out a nickel and gave it to Billy. The same minute he heard a chair scrape back from the table of drunks and a woman's too loud voice say, "Hey, none of that—none of that. He's my boy. Nobody can give my boy nickels but me!" A pudgy hand loaded with rings reached in front of Danny, clawed the nickel away from Billy, slapped it on the bar. Danny looked at the woman—bangs with gray in them, teeth wide apart in the loose mouth, too much rouge, big pores, eyes drunk and peevish. He watched while she put her arm through Billy's and staggered back to the table with him.

"What's that?" asked Danny.

"She ain't the Queen of Romania," said Roy, disgusted. "Hell, I don't know. Tourist trade. I never saw her before and hope I never do again. I get the screwiest customers in here." He shoved the glasses in a little group across the bar. "Give me a buck forty."

"Wait a minute."

Danny was watching the woman. She was holding a nickel back in one hand and shoving her drink at Billy with the other. "No drink, no nickels," she said to Billy. "You're my boyfriend. You got to drink with me."

It took Billy a while to get the idea, but finally he reached for the glass and raised it to his mouth. But before he could drink it Danny took it from his hand and set it down on the table.

"Lay off him," Danny said to the woman. He put a nickel in Billy's hand and pushed him away. "Just because he's deaf and dumb and got a mind like a baby don't give you the right to make fun of him. So lay off and keep your nickels to yourself."

"Who's talking?" asked a man at the table and started to get up. The woman turned on him. "Sit down, Dick, before you get your ears pinned back." She looked up at Danny and her mouth twisted on the question, "Whooryou?"

"No difference," said Danny.

"No difference," she repeated in a voice that sounded like a steam roller going over gravel. She grunted to herself and then raised her head. "Well, what is the difference? That's what I'd like to know."

"Lay off the kid."

The woman looked at him again, only different. "I thought they raised nothing but turnips in this country. Who raised you?"

"Not your mother." Danny began to move back toward the bar when the woman reached out and caught his wrist. "Aw," she said. "No hard feelings. Sit down and have a drink."

"I drink with my friends."

"You got a girl?" The woman peered up at him through bloodshot eyes. "Bring her over. We'll all get drunk together."

Danny hardly heard her. He was looking at the woman's hand on his wrist and, beyond her hand, the white cuff of his shirt. There was a stain on it. Not beer, not grease. A red stain, a stain like blood.

"She's out of your class," said Danny harshly. With his free hand he knocked over the highball glass and the woman pushed back her chair to keep the whisky off her lap. At the same moment Danny wrenched his other hand free and went over to the bar. "Take the drinks to the table, will you, Roy?"

The woman was still swearing at him, but Danny didn't even hear. He went to the end of the bar and through the door into the washroom.

He looked in the mirror above the washstand and for the first time that evening he saw his own face. It was like a shock—not because his face had changed, but rather because it hadn't. This was the same face that he'd seen every morning when he shaved and nobody else had noticed any change. He remembered now his surprise that people had recognized him when he came back from the killing on the path, that when he'd walked up to the bar a minute ago Roy had spoken to him just as he might have on any other night. That was the terrible thing, that something had happened, something that he alone knew, and yet nothing had changed. His face was the same, people acted the same as they had before. It was as though they were saying that what he had done was a lie, that it had happened in a dream. And for a minute he couldn't figure which was real—like those other dreams in which he spoke to a father he had never known, and who, he knew even when he talked to him, had been hanged long ago.

But it wasn't a dream. There was the little swelling under his right eye that felt sore when he touched it. There was the rip in his shirt hidden by his buttoned jacket. And on his right shirt cuff there was the spot of blood—no bigger than a dime, but it was blood. He'd better start moving before someone came into the washroom, better get home before the bruised eye turned black. He pulled down the cuff and rubbed soap into it and tried to wash it out but it still left a stain. Finally he reached for his knife to cut away the blood-marked cuff. The knife was gone.

Danny just stood there. He was still holding the broken piece of chain in his hand, trying to remember how he could have lost it in the fight, when he thought he heard somebody behind him. He looked up into the mirror, and there behind his own face was Billy Scripture's face, serious and kind of curious.

"How long you been standing there, Billy?" Danny said more to himself than to Billy.

For a moment longer they looked at each other's images in the mirror. All of a sudden Billy smiled.

Danny waited without moving until the other face had disappeared and he could hear Billy limping across the washroom. He put the loose end of the chain back in his pocket and rolled up the cuff so that it wouldn't poke out from his sleeve. Then he went back into the bar.

When he sat down at the table, Jimmy said, "I told you he was drunk. Look how white he is."

Danny felt very tired. "Drink up," he said. "We're going home."

"You're not sick, Daniel?" Gilly's voice was worried.

"No, I'm not sick," he answered. "I want to get back to town."

"You look drunk to me," said Jimmy. "I'm going to drive, by gosh."

Danny swallowed the glass of corn, feeling it burn down inside him like a rope of fire. When he got up, his chair fell back with a crash. "I'm going to drive," he said.

They were just getting off the porch when there was a streak of lightning over Bradford way, and the thunder came, like it was cracking the sky wide open. By the time they got into the car Danny could tell they were all scared. In the back seat Jimmy and Julie sat quiet together as if they were waiting for him to make a wrong move. Gilly looked at him, still worried, but her voice calm. "Sure you don't want Jimmy to drive?" she asked.

"Yes, I'm sure." He was breathing the cool air into his lungs and it braced him a little. He smiled at her. "What you scared about,

Gilly?"

She faced him quietly, then turned away. "Did I sound scared?"

"Didn't sound scared—but you are."

"Think nothing of it." She stopped talking on that one and Danny put the car into first.

When they left Roy's place the wind had begun throwing up little twisters of dust in the yard. On the road Danny could feel the gusts every time they hit the car and he could see the trees flailing around when the headlights passed them. In the dark sky the storm was piling up thick and every so often the lightning would flash, angry and white, behind the clouds. A second later they'd hear the thunder. It was almost as if Danny could feel the thunder—like it was something inside of him shaking a fist, beating to get out. And all he could do was bite his teeth together and put his foot down on the gas.

It wasn't long before the rain came down. Just a couple of big drops at first that spattered across the road and smacked his face through the open window. A minute later the rain was whipping across the windshield so thick the road just blurred into nothing. With the wipers it was a little better, but not much. Behind him he heard a voice. It was Jimmy leaning forward with his face near Danny's shoulder. "You're going too fast—you're going too fast," he said. "If we start skidding we'll never know what we hit."

"Still worried about your old man?" Danny asked. He looked down at the needle. It said sixty-five.

"I'm not worried about nothing but us," Jimmy begged. "Pull her down, will you, Danny? For gosh sakes!"

Gilly was looking straight ahead into the yellow blob of light where the headlights got lost in the rain. "Better listen to Jimmy," she said. "There's a railroad underpass up ahead somewhere."

Funny. He knew she was right. He knew Jimmy was right. But he couldn't stop. He had ninety wild horses under his foot and he was going to ride them all. It was as if maybe he wanted something to happen, or anyway was daring it to happen—because all of a sudden he felt like nothing could break him, like he was all rock and his head was a stone on his shoulders.

So it happened. Just like they said. He kept the needle right where it was even if he couldn't tell anymore where the macadam and the shoulder met. When he let up on the gas it was too late—he knew suddenly that he'd lost the road, that it wasn't up in front of him anymore, that it had twisted away to the right or left and was pitching down. He remembered the underpass, the narrow one with the wall in the middle dividing it into two lanes—like hitting a bull's-eye at three hundred yards. The next second he swung over the wheel, felt the road under the wheels again and they were sliding and screaming downward with the culvert dead ahead. Danny felt his heart stop beating during that endless time that he watched the black slit in the underpass come toward him like a hammer. He went in at an angle. He heard the back of the car slap against the concrete wall with the sound of steel flattening, then the other side, and they were out—rolling over against the embankment on the far side. Then the sedan stopped rolling and for a minute there wasn't anything but silence.

Behind him Danny heard the kids begin to cry like babies. The car was lying on its side and the only way out was up. Gilly was thrown against him as if she was dead or had fainted. He held her while he tried to push open the door above them. He climbed up and pulled her out. For a couple of minutes he'd forgotten all about Gilly, but now, now suddenly she was in his arms with the rain beating on her face. Finally her eyes opened and she looked up at him as if he was a stranger.

"Gilly," he said.

"It's all right, Daniel," she answered, her voice tired but not full of hate anymore.

And all of a sudden he was bent over, kissing her, and she didn't seem to care.

Chapter Two

Sunday night was quiet. The air was late September soft and over the Baptist Church steps the bottle flies were bouncing against the lamp shade with a little tinny sound. From where Danny stood across the street under the trees, he could hear the minister talking, but not the words he was saying—just a singsong sound that sometimes got louder and full of anger like the minister was tearing into the congregation for sinning, nothing special, but just general. It struck Danny funny that there were all those good folks catching heck for nothing in particular, and he, he was standing outside where he couldn't even hear what was being said. One of the damned, he thought.

He lit a cigarette and waited. He was thinking about Aunt Jessie who never hurt anything and never cheated anybody, sitting in the third row where she always sat, wearing that blue straw hat with the little flowers on it. Good old lady she was. Sometimes when he'd sit next to her he'd see her face for a minute, looking up at the minister kind of sad and worried as if everything he said was meant just for her and if the world was going to hell it was all her fault. He thought if Aunt Jessie had known about what happened— not the wreck, but what really happened—down at Brothers Pond the night before, she'd have taken the blame for that too.

He tried not to think about that, tried not to think about the storm and the water rising at the pond, tried not to think about the knife. Thinking was a sort of magnet, making him want to go back to Brothers Pond. He wanted to see if it was all true, like he remembered. He wanted to see if Jerry was still where he'd left him and he wanted to find the knife. Somehow, the night before, it hadn't seemed so important. Now he knew that if anybody found it, the sheriff would be looking for him in two hours. The knife might as well have had his name on it. It was a five-inch knife with a shaggy deer hide handle and a spring blade and he carried it because it was good on coon hunts. Jenkins' Hardware had never had more than one or two like it in stock.

But he knew he couldn't go back looking for the knife, not now, not for a while. There weren't going to be any more dances down at the pond till next summer and he didn't have any ordinary excuse for going down. All he could do was hope he'd dropped the knife in the water or someplace where nobody would see it. That was all he could do—hope. Anything else was dangerous.

About then he heard the congregation in the church get up and start singing "Lead, Kindly Light." He snapped the cigarette out into the road and stopped thinking about Brothers Pond. Suddenly he felt hot and tight inside and the muscles in his stomach got hard and stayed hard—like they did when he was trying to kill a pain somewhere. Only it wasn't pain he was feeling now. Then the hymn stopped and he heard the folks praying the benediction: *"The Lord watch between me and thee, while we are absent one from another."* The music had hardly died away when the doors opened and the folks came out, talking and shaking hands.

Right off he saw Gilly.

She was wearing a light yellow coat and no hat and she was alone. He watched while she went down the street under the elms and passed the second streetlight. He followed for a while on his side of the street before he crossed over. He walked up behind her and said her name, "Gilly …"

She broke step when she heard him. Then she looked up at him quick, but kept walking. "It's you, Daniel," she said. It didn't mean anything one way or the other. "You all right?"

"Sure," he said. "I was wondering about you."

"I'm all right." Her voice sounded cool and far away. He thought maybe she wanted to cry.

"You don't sound very happy," he said.

"Should I?" she asked. He didn't answer and they walked a little way in the darkness before she said, "Have you heard about Jimmy and Julie? I called Julie's house today but her mother wouldn't speak to me."

"Is that what's bothering you?"

"What do you think? All through service I could see everybody looking at me. I didn't have to look back. I could feel their eyes. I knew what they were thinking."

"Julie's just scared," Danny said. "Shock, the doctor called it. She vomits all the time. Jimmy's shoulder is broken—nothing else bad. They'll both be out of bed in a couple of weeks. Course the car ain't worth junk."

"It was my fault." Gilly sounded as if she were talking to herself. "That's what they were all thinking. I'm a schoolteacher, and I let it happen."

"Ain't nobody's fault," he said. "Anybody can have an accident."

"An accident?" Gilly raised her head in the dark and it seemed to him that her eyes looked at him kind of strange.

"What's wrong?"

She shook her head. "I don't think you'd understand."

"I can understand anything."

"You don't feel things. Why, the way you talk—"

"What do you know how I feel?"

"It doesn't make any difference." She turned away.

"It does make a difference," he said.

"Why?"

Danny waited a minute before he said it. "You and me. When parties are in love they got to understand each other."

"When—" she said and stopped. She shook her head like she couldn't believe what he'd told her. "What did you say, Daniel?"

"We're in love."

"You're crazy. Crazy."

"What was between you and Jerry Sykes?" He'd been wanting to ask her ever since he put his arms around her at the dance.

"I don't think that's any of your business."

"Maybe I can tell you."

"Tell me."

He watched her waiting. "The way I figure it, you're a girl from back yonder in the sticks, like me. Only you did better. Your folks didn't have a cent—sharecroppers they was, probably. But you had iron in your guts. You got yourself to a state school somewheres and worked twice as hard as everybody else. Then you come to this town all loaded up with education. And you're looking for a kill— somebody rich, somebody with a shiny red car as long as a hearse. Somebody like Jerry Sykes—with manners. Sure, he'd ask you for a dance. He's polite."

Gilly's face was drawn tight. "Is that all?" she asked.

"Only he ain't your kind, Gilly," he told her, feeling very sure of what he was saying. "I could tell your kind the first time you walked to school. You was scared stiff of the kids. You didn't even like Jerry Sykes. You liked what he had."

"I'll tell you about Jerry Sykes," Gilly said, her voice flat and sharp. "Jerry's the nicest boy I've ever known. Last night he asked me to marry him."

"And you said yes."

"Of course I said yes." She let that sink in before she went on talking. "And just because—because I went home with you rather than make a big scandal at the dance, Jerry's probably angry. I haven't heard a word from him all day."

"No?" Funny. He was suddenly surprised she hadn't.

Gilly turned when they got to the gate of the house where she boarded, a big wooden old-fashioned house with a porch and a lot of vines covering one end where the porch swing was. He saw the same look in Gilly's eyes that he'd seen before—like she was trying to size him up.

"You're strange," she said.

"You said that once before."

"But you are. Last night I thought you weren't drunk. Now I know you were. Are you always like that when you're drunk?"

"Like what?"

"Like—like—" She tried to put it in words. "Like you had a devil, or hate, in you. It made you do things."

"I was right. You were scared."

Gilly didn't pay any attention. "Why did you drive like that? It was like you wanted to kill yourself. All of us."

He grinned. "I like to hear the wheels go round."

"You're unhappy. That's it."

"You're smart, for a schoolteacher."

It was then that he heard a step on the sidewalk behind them and Gilly made a little move back as if she'd seen somebody she didn't want to see just that minute.

"Good evening, young people." It was Miss Simpkins, Gilly's boardinghouse-keeper.

"Good evening, Miss Simpkins," Gilly said.

"Didn't expect to see you up and about, Daniel." Miss Simpkins looked at him, holding her head straight back like a turkey.

"I'm all right, I reckon."

Miss Simpkins jerked her head a couple of times. "Well, it's like I told your Aunt Jessie at church tonight—it's a miracle any of you got out alive. Just a miracle." She went through the gate, past Gilly, and while she was walking toward the house she called back, "Try to come to church next Sunday, Daniel. We need young folks. It'll do you a heap more good than those dances at Brothers Landing."

Gilly waited until Miss Simpkins had gotten her key into the lock and gone inside. Then she turned to Danny. "Good night," she said.

"Good night?" he asked.

"Good night."

"I like you, Gilly."

Her voice was steady when she said, "I think I hate you."

"Which bedroom does old lady Simpkins sleep in?"

"At the top of the stairs. Why?"

"I'm going to sit on the porch swing with you."

"Don't you dare. It's bad enough her seeing us standing out here like this."

"I'm talking to you. What's wrong with talking?"

He opened the gate and started to go past Gilly toward the porch. She put her hand on his arm and stopped him. "Daniel," she said, "why did you wait for me outside the church tonight?"

"Why?" He looked at her. "I figured we might carry on where we left off."

"And where did we leave off?"

"Last night I kissed you."

"I should have slapped you."

"But you didn't."

"No—I didn't." She said it like it was a fact she didn't understand. At the step she tried to stop him again. "Daniel—please go."

"It's a nice evening—nice for talking." He put his hand on her arm. She pushed it away quick.

"Don't touch me," she said tensely. Her eyes searched his face as if to find the clue to a plea he would understand. "Don't you see or care? If this goes on I'll lose my job."

"Is that all you're worried about?"

He took her hand and she began to back away as he moved toward her. Then he pulled her against him. He wouldn't have cared if she slapped him or cursed him or anything she did. He tried to bring her face up to his, but she turned it to one side and his mouth touched the side of her cheek up toward the temple, near her hair. It smelled sweet and damp, and Gilly's body was close to his, fighting. And she kept whispering, "Let me go..."

"Gilly ...!"

And then suddenly something changed. She was still rigid against him—only different. He felt her face turn slow and hard so that his mouth moved across her cheek until her mouth was caught under his mouth and she was straining back at him with all the strength she had. And inside he felt suddenly quiet—like there was something he'd always wanted to know, and now he knew.

After a while she tore her mouth away and brought her face up close to his ear still holding tight. "Daniel," she whispered and her voice was scared and out of breath. "Where are we going? What are you doing to me?"

"This is what I want, Gilly. You. The hell with everything else."

And he heard her voice, still close up to his ear. "But what am I going to tell Jerry?"

What was she going to tell Jerry? That was a question. He walked back through the town and in his mind he kept coming back to what she'd said: "What am I going to tell Jerry?" He knew the answer all right, but he couldn't tell her. Jerry? You can forget about him, you can stop worrying what you're going to tell him.

Remember when they was playing "Put Your Arms around Me, Honey" and you were dancing with Saul Anderson? That was when Jerry Sykes took a powder—he went out of your life, out of mine, out of everybody's, even his own. Jerry's looking at the sky with his eyes wide open and he don't see nothing. There's low branches and grass bending over his face in the water, touching it when the wind blows, but he don't feel nothing. Jerry's deaf and dumb—like Billy Scripture. But he's dead, too. Dead, damn it, dead.

And he couldn't tell her. All he could do was look at her white face in the dark afterward and see tears wet on her cheeks and feel her trembling in his arms as if she was cold. He hadn't figured on this—on hurting her. He'd wanted to be nice to her, make her happy. But now he could see that it wasn't that simple, not for her, not for him. When he looked at her there was a word in his throat but he didn't know what it was and he couldn't say it. There was a hand in his stomach twisting, and he didn't know how to stop it. Only thing he did know was that in some crazy way it was Jerry Sykes that wouldn't leave them alone, that if Gilly was scared and mixed up it was because he was scared and mixed up too. For a minute a strange thing had happened. He got the idea she was crying for the man she didn't know yet was dead. And for a minute he wanted Jerry to be alive again so maybe he could give him back to her—if that was what she wanted—like you give a kid a toy.

It was past midnight and he stuck his hands in his pockets. His hands. But they weren't cold, they were sweating. The cold he felt wasn't the kind you could check with a thermometer; it was the kind you felt when you walked into a dark room and closed the door and suddenly you realized there was somebody in there with you, somebody you couldn't see. He began to watch the dark houses along the street—quiet, not a light, nothing moving. In those dark houses people were sleeping, and he had a queer feeling that there was something wrong about that, about them sleeping while he walked around awake—the killer. Those folks ought to be lying on their pillows with their eyes wide awake, listening to their hearts beat, thinking there was a killer free among them. But it was just the other way around. It was he that was scared and their sleeping that was the dangerous thing.

It bothered him—plenty. For twenty-four hours he'd been winning and nothing could stop him, but now he had a feeling the game was pulling out on him and in a way he couldn't understand. Everything had seemed clear the night before. Now it wasn't. He thought he'd finished something at Brothers Pond. Now, gradually, he began to know that it was only the beginning and that he was afraid to hear the end. The laugh, if any, was on him.

He thought the whole town was asleep but he found out different. It was on Main Street, the only place where they left the streetlights on all night. He had to go through Main Street to get to the other side of town where Aunt Jessie lived and he was just passing the Citizens' Bank when he saw somebody, a man, cross over at the far end under the last streetlight and come toward him. He didn't know why it gave him such a scare, but it did. It was the way it happened, the way they were all alone in the street walking toward each other. Almost without thinking Danny slowed down. He wanted to duck into a store entrance and hide till the other went past but he was afraid he'd already been seen. Then he noticed the man was limping a little.

It was Billy Scripture. Billy had a way of turning up anywhere, anytime—just because he had nothing else to do. After all his years in Bradford, Danny still didn't know who took care of Billy or who gave him his meals. But Billy hadn't missed a coon hunt with Danny and Mose for five seasons, and wherever he was he had some bright piece of junk in his hand, turning it over and over. Billy had an eye for anything with a shine to it. Seemed to give him a kind of pleasure.

As he came closer, Danny saw he was carrying something shiny now too, and for a split minute his mind went back to the washroom at Roy's with Billy looking over his shoulder while he was holding the broken knife chain in his hand. Only it wasn't the knife that Billy had, it was a broken piece of mirror. He seemed to be thinking to himself and Danny wondered if he was going to pass on by. But when Billy was nearly abreast, he lifted his head and grinned sudden to see Danny. He came across the sidewalk, bobbing his head happy-like. He pointed to the moon and lifted his head like a dog baying.

Danny patted him on the arm and nodded his head. "Sure, Billy," he told him. "We'll be hunting coon any night. You come with us."

Danny began to walk again before the other held him there any longer. The deaf mute stood there on the sidewalk watching him go. Halfway down the street Danny looked back, and he was still standing and watching. It was then that Danny began to wish that he knew better what kind of thoughts went through Billy Scripture's mind.

At last he was back in the dark streets again and felt better and didn't know why. Maybe it was the wind skittering through the trees just like it used to on the ridge back of his grandmother's place in Chinamook Valley. Listening to that sound in the branches he had the same feeling he used to have when he first came to Bradford, like being hungry for something he couldn't name, a kind of longing to get back to the valley and hear the wind roaring soft like waterfalls in the distance. The air was cold there too. In the mornings a trail of mist would straggle along the bottom of the valley above Chinamook Creek and then the shadow would climb up the side of Black Mountain, getting smaller and smaller as the sun came up, and finally you'd feel the sun on your face and your skin would be warm and cold at the same time.

It was empty, the valley was. Sometimes three or four days would go by without seeing a human being. The kind of folks you did meet talked slow and seldom, like they figured it was better to keep what they were thinking to themselves. Talking, Grandma used to say, gets complicated. But with all the scarcity of human beings, Danny had never felt really lonesome till he got among a townful of them. Back in Chinamook there were the things he was used to—Black Mountain that he'd seen every morning since he could remember, sounds he'd heard like a gray squirrel bustling through the leaves for chincapins, and smells like wood smoke from a morning fire. When he first came to Bradford he used to lie awake under the white starched sheets in his bed at Aunt Jessie's and all those sounds and smells would come to him and all he could do was tell himself that someday, someday he was going back.

That was what he told himself now. If things get too bad, he thought, I'll go back. I'll go back and everything will be simple like it was before. I won't be wondering what a deaf and dumb guy is thinking. I won't be afraid of a town that's asleep, putting ideas where there ain't any. I won't be telling myself that behind the dark windows in the houses folks are busy figuring who killed Jerry Sykes, standing behind the curtains watching me walk along the street at night. They're asleep, ain't they? If they thought I killed Jerry they wouldn't be sleeping, would they? Would they?

Then he turned in at Aunt Jessie's gate and the house was bright lit.

This is it, he told himself. They've found Jerry. They've found the knife. They've told Aunt Jessie and they're sitting in the parlor waiting for me. In a flash his mind went over the alibis: It ain't my knife or I must have lost it walking or I loaned it to somebody or I was there and saw the body and was afraid to tell anybody because they'd think I done it. Suddenly he knew he was caught, that he didn't have an excuse worth talking about, that the facts were plain as day. All he could say was: Sure, I killed Jerry Sykes last night at Brothers Pond. I hit him with a rock. I ain't sorry. I wish I was.

He got off the walk onto the grass and moved toward the house and up the porch steps, trying not to make any noise. From the top of the steps he could look through the big front window into the parlor but he couldn't see anybody—just Aunt Jessie sitting in the big rocker near the fish bowl still wearing her Sunday clothes. Her head was bent down and he couldn't tell whether she was thinking or sleeping. He waited till his breathing got more regular. He went in and closed the door easy behind him.

It didn't make any difference. Through the doorway between the parlor and the hall he heard Aunt Jessie's voice. "Daniel, is that you?"

"Yes, ma'am."

"It's late." Aunt Jessie sat in her chair looking tired. Her eyes were dark like they always were when she was worried about something.

He walked across the room and stood near the fish bowl. The speckled one waved his fins and began floating around in the water. His eyes always seemed like they were looking behind him.

"I was walking," Danny said.

"Till one o'clock?" According to Aunt Jessie, folks that weren't in their own houses by eleven o'clock were either coon hunting or out for sin.

"I went out to Mose's place to look over his dogs. It's near time for hunting."

Aunt Jessie smiled a little and when she spoke her voice was gentle. "You like hunting, don't you, Daniel? Coon hunting and squirrel hunting and woods and hills—the way it was when you were back in Chinamook with Grandma."

He didn't know what she had on her mind and he felt uneasy. "I don't know what you're driving at, Aunt Jessie," he said. "Sure I liked it back in the mountains. I was used to it, I reckon. But there ain't nothing there for me now, nothing except Grandma. I like it here all right."

"I wonder." Aunt Jessie stopped for a minute before she asked something else. "Have you heard anything from the railroad— when they're going to take you back to work?"

"I'll be on layoff for another three weeks anyways," Danny said. "You worried about my room rent?"

"No, Daniel," Aunt Jessie said softly. "It's just that a man needs something to keep him busy. Everybody does. Keeps them out of mischief, I guess."

"What're you talking about?"

Aunt Jessie looked at him kind of quick and smiled a little. "You, Daniel."

"Yeah—I do something?" He tried to keep his voice easy but the words sounded tight because his throat was tight.

"Sit down, Daniel—near me."

"I'd rather stand."

She didn't make anything of it. She folded her hands in her lap and hesitated before she said, "I'm afraid I haven't done very well by you, Daniel."

"What makes you think that?" He still couldn't figure what she was getting at or what she knew or how she'd gotten to know it.

"I guess I don't know very much about boys, Daniel. How can a person who's never had any children?" Aunt Jessie's voice sounded a little sad as if she were apologizing to him. "Ever since Grandma sent you to me, to see that you got some proper education, I've tried to do my best. And yet when I stop to think about it, I hardly know you. You come and go in the house and sometimes a week passes by without our hardly saying hello. Except for Mose, I don't know who your friends are or what you do. Sometimes I think I might as well have a boarder, a stranger."

"Nobody ever asked me where I was coming or going, Aunt Jessie. I ain't been used to explaining."

"That isn't what I want, Daniel. It's something else and I hardly know how to tell you. It isn't good for a boy never to have known his own—" Aunt Jessie's voice got a little strained here as if there was something she was ashamed to talk about—"his own pa and ma."

"Why don't you say it?"

Aunt Jessie looked up at the sudden anger in Danny's voice.

"About Pa—about him shooting a man and being hung for it—" The words tasted bitter in his mouth.

Aunt Jessie was quiet for a minute and her face looked gray in the light from the lamp. She smoothed her dress very carefully across her lap and said, "That is something I have never talked about."

"Why?" Danny's words poured out of him. "Why is everybody afraid to talk about it? It's like they're saying it was his fault, all that happened, that Pa was guilty and no questions asked. And that's what you're saying by not saying anything—you're saying that my pa ought to have had done to him what they did, that they ought to have hung him—"

"Jeb was my brother," Aunt Jessie said very quiet. "I think he had a lot of right on his side. All the same he done wrong." She waited a minute before she went on. "But that was over and done long ago, Daniel—even before you can remember. It's your life I'm talking about now. You've always been apart, kind of—like you were afraid of folks or didn't trust 'em. If you're going to live among people, Daniel, you got to trust them."

Suddenly Danny remembered the dark streets and the windows and the sick fear in his stomach. "What give you these ideas just now, Aunt Jessie? Why you talking like this?"

"It's just—well, when you first came you were such a shy, quiet boy, and somehow, without me hardly knowing it, you've grown up and you've changed. People talk to me. They say you're wild—"

In the fish bowl the speckled one had stopped swimming and just floated in the water, motionless. "Who's been talking to you?" Danny asked.

He could see it bothered Aunt Jessie to talk about it. "Jimmy Biff's father spoke to me after church tonight. He says that wreck last night—it was your fault."

"How come he made that conclusion?"

"Jimmy said you were drunk."

"Jimmy lied."

What he said, and the way he said it, must have confused her some because she didn't seem to know exactly what to say next. "Well—perhaps he did," she said. "Perhaps he did." Aunt Jessie shook her head. "I don't understand it, Daniel—you're getting a bad name but you don't seem to care about it."

"I reckon I don't," he said. "What else he tell you?"

"That was all." Aunt Jessie looked like she was trying to understand. After a while she said, "But hasn't it ever come into your mind that when you do these things it is bad enough what you are doing to yourself—but what about the other people?"

"What other people?"

"My heavens, there are those two children, little Julie and Walter Biff's boy. And that schoolteacher who was with you, Miss Johnson—"

Danny looked up. "What about her?"

"Why, she may lose her job. If she can't keep young people in hand a little better, why she wouldn't make a very good schoolteacher. Jimmy told Mr. Biff that she had a drink like everybody else."

"She didn't have anything to do with the wreck. The car just skidded, that's all. It could have happened to anybody."

"Well, Daniel, I hope that is all there was to it." Aunt Jessie got up and stood there, kind of tired and sad because she hadn't managed to settle anything anyway with all her talk. She put her hand on his arm, kind of awkward like she was a little afraid to do it. "I know you're not a bad boy, Daniel," she said. "Nothing anybody could tell me would make me think different. Even in spite of all that might have happened long ago, there hasn't ever been a drop of bad blood in our family and you couldn't help but be a good boy. And that's what I told Walter Biff."

That last thing she said took Danny completely by surprise. It put a quick hard thing in his throat and all he could say was, "That was right nice of you, Aunt Jessie, right nice."

She looked up into his face. "After this, Daniel, let's talk together a little more often. Yes?"

"Yeah. Sure, Aunt Jessie. Sure."

"And now kiss me good night."

That was the hardest thing Aunt Jessie ever asked. For a minute he wondered if he had the strength to do it, to break the iron rod in his back. He wasn't a kid, a baby. He didn't say his prayers. He never did. It was like being ashamed in the heart, ashamed and afraid that if he let go he'd never be able to hold himself so straight again.

Finally she patted his arm and moved away and said good night and he wished he'd done that little thing she'd asked. But all he could do was stand there angry with himself, angry that this was the way things were and it was too late to change them, and finally hearing her voice as she went toward the stairs, "There's a button missing on your coat, Daniel. Remind me in the morning. I'll sew one on for you."

He didn't know how long he stood there after he heard Aunt Jessie's bedroom door close—just stood there, not thinking, not moving, like the speckled fish in the bowl, and his heart like a heavy hammer. When he got upstairs to his room he shut the door and leaned against it. He felt more tired than he'd ever felt before and it was a minute before he could get out a handkerchief and wipe the sweat from his face. It wasn't his handkerchief. It was Gilly's, sweet-smelling, still cool damp with her tears. How long was it since he'd left her? An hour? It could have been a hundred years.

He went to the window and opened it and felt the cold air sting his face and neck. There wasn't a light in Bradford anywhere— just a late moon shining over the bare trees in the back yards. Everything was quiet and still, like it wasn't a town where people would wake up next morning and go to shops or stores or banks. It was like a town that'd been dead a long time.

I got to get things clear, he thought. I got to arrange the facts. If I don't, anything can happen. And he told himself: The town's asleep and it don't know anything. Billy Scripture's got a brain like a baby and he don't know. Aunt Jessie thinks there's not a bad drop of blood in the family and she don't know. There ain't but one person in this whole town that knows who killed Jerry Sykes and that's me.

Suddenly it came over him that that was the most awful thing of all.

Chapter Three

First person he saw next morning was Ken Williams, the guy who led the band at the Brothers Pond dances. He was all alone at the counter of Billy's Drug, eating ham and eggs and looking through *Downbeat* magazine. Ken and Elmer, the soda jerk, must have been carrying on some kind of running talk when Danny came in because Elmer was leaning across the counter asking questions in a low excited voice and Ken was answering him while he flipped the pages of the magazine.

They both looked up when Danny came in. "Hello, Hawkins," said Ken. "You all right?"

"I'm all in one piece."

Ken half smiled while he looked at Danny. "I hear you went for a ride Saturday night—thought you were on the Indianapolis Speedway."

"I thought I was on a road—but I wasn't."

"Didn't somebody get hurt—Jimmy Biff and Julie what's-her-name?"

Elmer leaned across the counter looking at Danny as if he were a hero. "Honest, you didn't break a leg or nothing happen to you?"

"Not a scratch."

Ken spoke up. "Then who handed you that shiner?"

Danny looked at Ken and grinned. "The dashboard hit me."

"Doggone!" said Elmer. "It's a doggone miracle. To be in a wreck like that and come out with only a shiner. And right on top of Jerry Sykes taking a powder—boy, the town's jumping!"

"What about Jerry Sykes?" Danny asked.

"He's disappeared, took a powder," Elmer said. "Ain't nobody seen him since Saturday night. Ask Ken—he drove his car back after the dance."

Ken was spreading jam on a piece of toast. "That's all," he said. "I just drove his car home. I came out after the place closed and

Jerry's red Buick was still sitting there. Must have been near four o'clock in the morning. I figured he must have got plastered and gone home with somebody else."

"Yeah," said Elmer. "He does them crazy things sometimes. I remember once —"

Danny wanted to stay on the subject. "Anybody see him leave?" he asked.

"Guess not," said Ken. "One of the boys in the band says Jerry went to the men's room and didn't come back—but he can't remember what time of evening it was. You were down at the dance, Hawkins. Notice anything?"

"Once on the dance floor I saw him. He was with Gilly Johnson."

"That's right."

"Say, Ken," Elmer broke in, "you don't suppose he went in swimming and, jeez, you don't suppose—"

"Not unless he went naked. His bathing suit was in the car."

"Well, there's gotta be some explanation," Elmer said, then lowered his voice. "Can it, you guys!"

Danny looked into the mirror back of the counter and saw Jerry's father, old J. B. Sykes, standing near the door, looking fat and worried.

"Where's the papers?" he asked Elmer.

"The *Dispatch* ain't come in yet, Mr. Sykes. Probably be in on the ten-ten."

J. B. nodded in a nervous kind of way, like he was thinking of half a dozen things at once. His eye fell on Ken. "Hello, Williams," he said. "Haven't heard anything, have you?"

"No sir, Mr. Sykes, I haven't." Ken wiped his mouth with a napkin.

"Going down to the pond?"

"Soon as I finish breakfast," Ken told him.

J. B. stood there for a minute longer, just nodding his head without much sense. He looked kind of surprised and bewildered, like a pig when it's just been stunned by the back of an ax. It seemed as if for the first time in his life something had happened that he didn't know how to handle right off, and he wasn't used to it. For half a second his eyes caught Danny's in the mirror and Danny could see that he was almost at the point of asking him if he knew anything about Jerry. But he must have figured that Danny didn't because he turned without saying anything more and went out.

Ken and Elmer watched him go. "Jeez," Elmer said, "old J. B. looks plenty worried. Bet he didn't sleep a wink last night." He turned back to Ken. "You know, there's gotta be an explanation!"

Ken got off the stool and reached into his pocket. "Gilly Johnson went home in your car," he said to Danny. "That's funny. She came with Jerry. What made her walk out on him?"

Elmer looked up and snapped his fingers like he'd just hit a big clue. "Jeez, yeah—what about it, Danny?"

"Maybe she got tired of waiting," Danny said. After a pause he added, "Anyway, he'll probably show up in a day or two—probably sleeping it off somewheres. Maybe he went to Richmond."

"Why should he go to Richmond?" Ken asked. He peeled a twenty-dollar bill from a roll and laid it on the counter.

When Elmer saw the money he almost forgot what they were talking about. "Holy cow," he said, "look at that roll of dough. Enough to choke a horse. Look at it, Danny!"

Ken seemed kind of annoyed at all the attention. "What's the matter?" he asked pretty sharp. "Haven't you ever seen any folding money?"

"Not that much," said Elmer.

Ken watched him for a second and then smiled. "Tuition money, you sap. What you think I wave that stick for all summer?"

Elmer looked like the sight of all that money had made him unhappy at just being a counter boy. "Listen, Ken," he said, "if I get a trumpet will you give me a job in your band and take me to New York—if you ever go to New York?"

"First you got to learn to blow it," said Ken. He folded *Downbeat* magazine and stuck it in his pocket. "Want to go down to the pond with me, Hawkins? They're going to try grappling—"

Danny held his coke in his hand. "I reckon not," he said.

"I reckon," Ken said after him. "I reckon. When you going to stop talking like hillbilly white trash, Hawkins?"

After the screen door slammed shut Danny sat there holding the coke in his hand, not even daring to set it down, for fear he'd break the glass. When he raised his eyes he caught Elmer staring at him with just a bit of a smile on his face, and a look in his eye like he was half remembering something.

"What you know," Elmer said. "Excitement! I tell you anything can happen in this town!"

He began to clear away Ken's dishes and he seemed to be thinking to himself again. After a while he turned to Danny and said, "I bet you clear forgot the time Jerry Sykes trimmed you."

"Jerry never trimmed me."

"Sure he did. Back of the school—first day you started. Remember?"

"We had a fight—if that's what you're talking about."

"He trimmed you." Elmer's fat, dumb face didn't change expression a bit. He said it like it was a fact. "I never could figure it. You had it all over him, but he trimmed you—like you was scared to fight. What for?"

"You're crazy if you think Jerry ever scared me."

"I was one of the guys got Jerry to fight you."

"I know you were."

"But I didn't have nothing to do with what happened the night after. Tarring was Jerry's idea—said you was yellow."

"Don't make no difference now."

"No, guess it don't." Elmer stared out of the window at the street for a minute. "He was a heller, Jerry was. Funny thing, I put Jerry onto you, but I was hoping you'd trim him that day back of the school. I didn't like him, never did. It was the way he acted, like his old man was J. B. Sykes and it give him more rights than other guys. I never did see that just because your old man was a criminal it was any sign that—"

"Here." Danny put a nickel on the counter so sudden it stopped Elmer from saying anything else. "You talk too much."

"Jeez!" Elmer looked like he was really sorry. "I didn't mean—heck, I guess you're right. I do talk too much."

"Forget it."

Elmer did. He picked up the nickel, and while Danny was moving to the door he called after him, "Hey, Danny—you suppose Ken was serious about me and the trumpet?"

"I wouldn't know."

He went out into the sunshine and didn't look back because he was afraid Elmer might be watching him through the window. Elmer wanted to know if he remembered. Sure he remembered— he remembered everything, the walking across the playground in his squeaky shoes that first day not knowing that already everybody knew his father had been hung. He remembered being shoved and seeing Jerry Sykes for the first time, the kids crowding around while they fought, the weakness in his arms because he was scared, not of Jerry, but of all that pack of hollering, grinning kids. He remembered the night after, how they'd caught him and ripped off his clothes and held him while Jerry smeared tar over his body, and how he'd hid shivering and naked in the alley for three hours before he dared run home. And he remembered how Willard Peake, the truant officer, had come to take him back to school a week later. "Oughtn't to take it so serious, boy," Willard had told him. "Got to forget these things. Kids are kids." That was an easy word, forget. Easy to say.

It was near train time and Danny walked along Main Street toward the station. A couple of men were hanging a big street banner about the county fair between the Citizens' Bank and the Lodge Building, but nobody was paying much attention to them except a few farmers who'd done their business and were just loafing around before they drove home. Red Harris didn't have any customers yet and he was sitting in his own barber chair staring through the window at folks passing by. Judd Jenkins was sweeping the sidewalk in front of his hardware store across from the courthouse, and down the street there was the usual crowd waiting for the morning mail to be sorted.

Everything was the same as always, slow and nothing much happening—nothing unusual, that is. And yet to Danny the town seemed different that morning, dreamlike—only a bad dream where everybody moved slow and talked on street corners in the sun and waited for the mail but you knew that something terrible was going to happen. That slowness was a lie, everything was a lie, and even the sunshine wasn't real and had a kind of darkness in it. It seemed like he was being tricked and wasn't sure of anything anymore, like he was suddenly color-blind and the red brick of the Citizens' Bank had turned black. He wanted to walk naturally, but one minute it seemed he was walking too fast and then he was walking too slow. Even noises were tricky. Somebody hollered across the street and it sounded like it was miles off. But once when somebody said his name next to him, it went off in his ear like a shotgun. He looked down at the man on the bench, down at the silver star hung loose on his vest. "Hello, Sheriff," he said.

They were all there as usual, sitting on the bench on the station platform, waiting for the trains to come in—Sheriff Clem Otis and Homer Blackstone and Ed Conlon and Uncle Joe Jingle, not one of them a day under sixty. Uncle Joe was so old he'd blown a bugle at Appomattox and he still wore his Civil War campaign hat. Clem had been sheriff ever since he got a game leg out of a freight wreck up Roanoke way. Ed and Homer were both retired off the railroad and now there was nothing left for them to do but sit down at the yards and criticize the engineers and spit. Homer claimed that, allowing for wind direction and speed, he could put a gob of tobacco juice on a fly ten feet away four times out of five, but nobody had ever seen him do it.

Clem looked up at Danny out of the corner of his eye. "Made you jump, eh, feller? Got to be careful. You'll wear out your brain thinkin'."

"I was looking for a guy. The freight from Tidewater in yet?"

"I think she's sitting over in the yard now. Who you looking for?"

"Mose Jackson."

"Goin' huntin'?"

"Guess so—pretty soon anyway."

"High type feller, that Mose, ain't he? Engineer says he can read as good as anybody."

"Better. He's read about every book there is, I reckon."

Clem shook his head. "That's too much."

Uncle Joe was watching them talk. "Who's that boy?" he asked.

Clem raised his voice and bent toward Uncle Joe. "It's Jessie Hawkins' boy—her nephew. Folks ain't livin'. She brung him up."

"Who?"

Clem raised his voice again. "Daniel Hawkins. That's his name."

Uncle Joe looked at Danny for a minute, almost suspicious. "Ain't Yankee?"

Clem laughed. "No, God. He's from Chinamook, the mountains."

"White trash."

"My granddaddy fought at Chattanooga Mountain," Danny said. "I got his musket to prove it."

Clem leaned toward Uncle Joe. "He says his granddaddy fought at Chattanooga Mountain."

"Tell him to sit down," said Uncle Joe.

Danny hadn't felt like talking and when he'd first seen Clem wearing the badge he'd had all he could do to keep from running. It still gave him a funny feeling, seeing that star hung on Clem's vest, but somehow he'd begun losing the feeling that everything was a dream. It was comfortable the way the old fellows talked, comfortable and friendly, so he sat down and listened and watched the freight cars being shunted around the yard till 849 blew her whistle coming into the block.

"Was that 849 blowin' just then?" Homer asked.

"I reckon," said Danny.

Clem took out his watch and looked at it. "Seven minutes late," he said. "They ought to whip that engineer."

"Who's driving her?" asked Homer.

"Cal Wheaton. He couldn't make a dog run."

They watched the train come in on number one track, ringing her bell and blowing steam out the side. Cal leaned out of the window of the cab and waved. A fellow kicked a couple bundles of papers out of the baggage car as she went by. Finally she stopped and a few folks started getting on and off. The old guys sat on the bench, watching and making cracks about who was getting off the train. Uncle Joe asked, "Who's that feller just got off?"

"Drummers," said Ed Conlon. "You could sell anything in this town."

"I didn't say two fellers. I said one feller," said Uncle Joe, kind of peeved. "The feller with the little satchel and the black suit."

"Where?"

"Yonder." Uncle Joe lifted the hand with the cane. "Third car. You blind?"

It was then that Danny saw the little man coming toward the station from the far end of the platform. He was carrying a leather satchel like lawyers carry papers in and he wasn't much over five-foot-four. But that wasn't what made him especially peculiar. It was the clothes he was wearing—black suit, black shoes, black tie, black hat. It made his face seem even whiter than it was.

The four old guys on the bench didn't move an eye off the little man. "What do you make of him?" asked Ed Conlon.

"I dunno," said Clem.

"Mebbe a lawyer," said Homer. "Mebbe some rich Yankee sent him to buy Blackwater plantation."

Clem grunted. "Blackwater ain't for sale—never was, never will be as long as old Lizzie Wilder's alive."

"Well, he ain't a drummer."

"There's only three kinds of people wear a black suit like that," said Ed positively. "Preachers, undertakers, and detectives."

"Bradford don't need any more preachers and undertakers," said Homer. "And what use would we have for a detective?"

Clem was watching the little man as he came closer. "Curious sort of human being, ain't he?" he said.

The stranger walked past the men on the bench, looking around like he expected to find someone waiting for him. Finally he went to the waiting room door. He had his hand on it when Clem looked up and said, "Ain't no telephone in there, mister."

The man stopped, undecided.

"Cab driver ought to be here soon—always is at train time."

The stranger waited a minute longer. Then he turned and walked back down the platform.

"Talkative cuss," said Homer, squinting after him. "Mebbe Ed's right," said Clem. "Mebbe he is a detective."

At the end of the station the stranger turned and walked around the corner of the building, like he'd seen whoever he was looking for. Danny got up and went through the waiting room and crossed to the window where he could see the parking space on the other side. There was a big black sedan sitting out there and, while he watched, old J. B. Sykes got out and hurried toward the stranger. He took the satchel from the little man and carried it back to the car for him.

"Well, I'll be hung for a witch!" Danny heard Clem's voice behind him. "Never thought I'd see the day when old J. B. would carry anything for anybody."

"Must be an important guy."

"What in tarnation could J. B. need a man like that for—a man so important he wears nothing but black and carries papers with him. Now there's something to figure!"

By the time Danny got down to the roundhouse Mose had checked in his gear and gone. He watched them put a new boiler in an engine while he tried to make up his mind what to do. He thought about going home and lying in his room at Aunt Jessie's until evening, waiting till there might be some word from the grappling crew at Brothers Pond, waiting till he could meet Gilly at the culvert outside of town. But he knew that was no good, waiting—that he had to keep moving. Moving was a protection against going crazy, against telling. When he stopped or stood still he had thoughts he was afraid of—like how easy it would be to walk down Main Street and stop the first person he saw, anybody, and tell them where Jerry was, not at the bottom of the pond where the grappling hooks would find him, but at the edge under the branches. That was the easy way of making everything simple. Too easy.

When he looked up he had already walked three miles away from town and he was on the hot dirt road with dusty, dead sumac growing along the edge. Up ahead, through the locust trees and the brambles that had spread over everything, stood Blackwater mansion, and behind it the abandoned slave quarters where Mose lived. There had been a time, folks said, when the plantation covered half of Bradford County and took in all the bottom land and swamp clear to Brothers Pond. But that was during Civil War times when Lizzie Wilder was a little girl and her father was a colonel in the Confederate Army. For years now, Lizzie had been living at an old ladies' home in Richmond, while the taxes cut the property down to nothing but the house and the swamp, and the old mansion itself just rotted and fell apart year after year. Even the furniture still stayed just as Lizzie had left it—rooms full of gold-framed mirrors, French engravings, and four-poster beds—but dirty now, covered with cobwebs and rat trails. Couple of times rich Northerners had tried to buy the place, but Lizzie wouldn't even talk to them—said she was going to leave Blackwater as a memorial to what the Yankee did to the South. The only person she'd let live on the place all these years was Mose—"Left me here, I guess, just so no damn Yankee'd ever steal the place," Mose said.

Danny found him out in the pen behind his shack, feeding the hounds corn mush and meat scraps. The dogs were yelping and jumping all over Mose and he didn't even notice anybody had come until Danny lifted the latch and came inside the chicken wire.

"Listen to Mister Dog," said Mose. He was big and his voice was like a big man's—deep and slow. "No manners. No manners at all."

"Maybe you don't feed them enough," Danny said.

Mose grunted. "Feed them too much and they get fat in the belly and want to sleep all the time. Stop being keen." He emptied the bucket into the last trough and looked at Danny. "How you been?"

"I'm all right. I figured I'd find out when we might go hunting for coon."

"I don't know," Mose said. "Couple fellows from the lodge asked me yesterday to take them out. I told them maybe Friday if the air stays sharp."

"Going to carry them back?"

"Carry nothing," said Mose. "I told them—you get tired and you walk back on your own feet. Aren't any trucks going to pick you up when your feet get sore." Mose shrugged his shoulders. "I don't particular like to take those fellows out, but the dogs got to earn their keep somehow. Railroading isn't going to feed Mister Dog."

"Mister Dog," Danny said. "Why you call everything mister?"

For a minute Mose looked at Danny out of the corner of his eye, like he had a joke and was making up his mind whether to let Danny in on it. "Isn't enough dignity in the world," Mose said, and jerked his head toward the shed. "Come here. I got something to show you."

Danny followed the Negro into the shed. It was dark and musty in there and for a minute he couldn't see anything. As his eyes got used to the dark, he saw something over in one corner, a hound bitch lying in the straw and something wriggling around her belly.

"Daisy Bell," said Danny.

"Littered over two weeks ago. Eight of them and only one died. She's done her duty by the dog race."

The puppies were crawling over each other trying to find a teat—brown-spotted, all skin and paws and wet black muzzle for sucking milk. Danny knelt down in the straw and held one of them in his hands before Daisy Bell got up and shook off the pups. She moved in close to Danny and waited for him to scratch her throat and nip her ear. "I'll be doggoned, Daisy Bell," said Danny. He felt good, like he wanted to laugh. "I'll be doggoned. Look what you went and done." He looked up at Mose. "Who's pappy?"

"Juniper," said Mose. "I never saw such a disgusted dog—just came in next morning, took one sniff and made a very rapid departure." Mose chuckled to himself. "Just like a man dog. He done it but he don't want any part of it."

"How you know it was Juniper?"

"How I know it was Juniper? I could have told you if I hadn't mated them on purpose. Just the way he acts."

"What you mean—the way he acts?"

"Guilty, guilty as hell. Always tell when Mister Dog done something he shouldn't, like killing a chicken. He comes up to you too cheerful entirely, wagging his tail. Or he runs away from you with his tail between his legs. All means the same thing." Mose started out of the shed. "Course tying up with a female isn't exactly high crime and misdemeanor. It's just that starting a family—well, it makes a dog feel plain ridiculous."

Danny was thinking about what Mose had said first. "How's he know what's good and what's bad?"

"Same as folks—somebody told him." Mose looked at Danny out of the corner of his eye again. "What's the matter, Daniel—in a philosophical mood, aren't you?"

"Not particular."

"Seems to me you're kind of serious."

They left the kennel and walked back toward Mose's shack. Mose appeared to be thinking to himself and Danny was quiet too, trying to find words for something he wanted to tell Mose. After a while he said, "I got me a girl, Mose."

Mose stopped short. "What's that?"

"I got me a girl."

"Uh-huh. That's what I thought you said." Mose began walking again.

"Ain't you interested?"

"Guess so," said Mose, without looking at Danny. "What you going to do about it?"

"I don't know." Danny waited for a minute before he went on. "I only seen her twice—to talk to, I mean. I got to have her."

Mose shrugged his shoulders. "Don't need my permission," he said. "What's the matter? She don't like you?"

"I think maybe she's afraid," Danny said slowly, as if he was just realizing it himself for the first time.

"Afraid because of what happened to your pappy?"

"I don't know." Danny waited again and then the question came out of him. "What if she's right? What if everybody's right about Pa? What if there's bad blood in me—makes me do bad things?"

Mose stopped again at the stoop of his shack and looked at Danny, almost as if he were angry. "I don't know what you're talking about—bad blood. Blood is red, keeps you alive—it don't tell you what you got to do."

Mose pushed back his trainman's cap so the crinkly gray hair showed above his ears. He looked off toward the swamp that began at the end of the lane running between the two rows of slave shanties. "Tell you something, Daniel," he said after a minute. "I found a bum sleeping in a boxcar once on the run down from

Roanoke. I was brakeman then and by rights I should have kicked him off. But there was something about the way he was lying there and the way his face looked while he was sleeping that made me change my mind. He looked cold too, so I threw his coat over him and left him there sleeping. Next time I see him he's in the county jail for trying to make love to a girl that turned out to be the constable's daughter. First I heard of it was when the sheriff grabs my dogs to chase him. Little guy's still trying to run away when the dogs are all over him and he's shot in the leg and as soon as they can hold a trial he's sent to jail for fifteen years. You think he was bad? You think what he done was worth fifteen years?"

"He was guilty, wasn't he?"

"Guilty? That's what Mister Law wrote on the books. But guilty of what? Guilty of wanting a little loving. They give him fifteen years for being lonesome—not for having bad blood." Mose frowned as if it made him sad and angry to remember it. "Never did feel right about the sheriff using the dogs. It's all right for a dog to hunt a coon—but not a man."

After a while Danny said kind of quiet, "You get lonesome, don't you, Mose—living here with your back to the swamp—but you don't commit no crimes."

"Sure I get lonesome," Mose said heavily. "Man ought to have a woman, friends anyway. Man ought to live in a world with other folks. Man gets tired talking to himself, gets tired watching the fireflies and listening to the night and the frogs bellowing in the swamp. When I come out here I thought I'd be out of the way and nobody would shove me around because of my color. What I did was resign from the human race—and I guess that's about the worst crime there is—" Mose's voice was suddenly deep with bitterness. "Only they don't hang you for it," he said.

Mose stood there for a minute before he went up the step, his face bitter and sad. Then he looked kind of sharp at Danny. "Anyway, what's all this talk about good and bad? What's it got to do with your girl? You done something makes you ashamed?"

Danny lifted his eyes and answered quickly, "Oh, nothing. Nothing in particular, I reckon."

Danny took out his Ingersoll watch and brought the tip of his cigarette close to the dial to read the time. Gilly had said she'd be at the culvert at nine o'clock and she was twelve minutes late already. For over an hour he'd been walking back and forth in the road, pulling out the watch and discovering that the little hands on the dial had only moved ahead five minutes, eight minutes, three minutes. Nearly as often he had strained his eyes toward the bend in the dirt road where Gilly would come, thinking he saw someone, but always it was his mind that had tricked him. Once a car had come down the road from the direction of town and Danny had crept down under the culvert and heard it pass overhead. When he came up on the road afterward the dust still hung in the air.

It was almost as if the air were asleep—nothing moved. In the thick darkness sounds came from uncertain distances—the crickets, the frogs croaking in the swamp, even the sound of his own footsteps in the soft dust of the road. Now and then he would lean over the culvert wall and down below, almost as if it were the murmur of a seashell, he heard the brook sliding through the culvert and down toward the swamp. It was good, the dark was—safe. And when he thought of Gilly coming to meet him in the dark he stopped feeling afraid or lonely. He could feel sorry for Mose, lying in his shack reading books all night and willing to give them all up just to have a woman that belonged to him. He could even feel sorry for the tramp who'd made the pass at the constable's daughter and got fifteen years for it. Then he thought of Jerry lying at the edge of Brothers Pond. He was loneliest of all.

It was an odd thing about Jerry. Danny was beginning not to hate him anymore. He wondered if maybe talking to Mose had changed it—all that talk about people not being bad but just afraid and lonely. Danny couldn't quite figure it yet. It was easier to say a man was guilty and give him fifteen years, it didn't take so much thinking. But there was a way that Mose said things—slow and soft and deep—that made you listen, made you believe him, made you feel gentler inside, like he was. But whatever the reason was,

Jerry had changed when he thought of him. It wasn't the mean narrow face with the tight thin mouth that Danny saw when he remembered. It was Jerry's face the way he'd left him on Saturday night—a kid's face, it was, helpless, and when he was dead his face showed how hard he was still trying to live. Somehow he wasn't an enemy of Danny's anymore. Not a friend, but not an enemy either.

Those are dangerous thoughts, Danny told himself. First thing I know I'll be sorry for Jerry Sykes and then I won't know where I stand. He swung his legs off the culvert and started across the road. Abruptly he stopped. It seemed as if he'd heard a footstep up the road—but again there was nothing but the darkness and the sound of the crickets and the frogs. What's keeping her? he thought, and then something frightened him. What if she wasn't coming at all? What if they'd found Jerry Sykes and the knife and already they were looking for him? What if Gilly had heard the news and already she knew that Danny had killed Jerry and hated him for it? What if Gilly was helping them—she knew where Danny would be, at the culvert. What if she came, just to lead the sheriff to where he was?

Then he saw Gilly walking toward him out of the dark.

He just stood there not even watching her, but watching the road behind her and the trees along the side of the road. When he looked down she was standing in front of him, her hair loose on her shoulders, her light coat buttoned at the neck.

"You alone?" he asked.

"Yes," she said slowly, as if she didn't know what he meant. She put her hand on his arm. "You're trembling, Danny."

For a minute longer he wasn't sure—then he believed her, believed she was alone. "I been waiting since eight o'clock," he said.

"I told you nine."

"I know," he said, impatient without knowing why. "Let's walk."

For a little while they walked along the road away from town, not saying anything. Danny wanted to reach out and take Gilly's hand, but right then she wasn't saying anything, either. She seemed a long way off, cool and thinking her own thoughts—and he was too proud to bring her back by touching her. He wanted her to come back, of her own will.

At last she said, "I know now why Jerry didn't call me Sunday."

"Something happen?" Danny asked. His throat was dry.

"He hasn't been home since the dance at Brothers Landing. Nobody's seen him."

"Yeah. I know."

Gilly looked up in surprise. "You knew?"

"I saw Ken Williams this morning at Billy's Drug."

"Oh …"

"You worried?"

"I hope nothing happened to him. He was drunk and had all that money on him."

"Is that what you been thinking about all the time we been walking?"

"I suppose so," Gilly said quietly.

Jealousy made Danny's voice hard. "You in love with Jerry?"

Gilly gave a little laugh but there wasn't any enjoyment in it. "With Jerry? How could I be?" She stood still in the road and put her hands over her eyes and shook her head. "Oh, Danny," she said, her voice full of unhappiness. "I don't know anything, anything at all. I don't even know why I'm seeing you, why I'm meeting you in dark places where people won't see us—as if we were hunted or criminals. I feel as if I were in a long dark tunnel and didn't know where I was coming out."

"I thought you liked me."

"I do—I do," Gilly said. "Even more, maybe, but it's almost as if you were stronger than me, or that something was pulling me toward you, something I can't trust. To like somebody ought to make you feel quiet inside too, but I don't feel quiet. And you"—she looked up at him—"sometimes I think that when you're with me you're not really happy, not really happy."

"How you figure that?"

"Because you're not quiet inside either. It's in your eyes, the way you hold yourself—a strain."

He didn't answer. Instead he started moving, and Gilly turned too and walked beside him. After a while she asked, "Where we going?"

"Blackwater."

"Isn't that where Mose lives?"

"He's out in back. He won't know we're there."

He was still walking straight ahead, cold, the muscles hard and tight across his stomach. Gilly stopped.

"Danny—"

He turned back to her. "What?"

"Why don't you tell me—" she asked, looking up at him as if she were a child asking forgiveness. "Why don't you tell me that I'm wrong or crazy or just upset—that there's nothing to be afraid of?"

And suddenly it was as if the hand inside him had opened and let go and when he answered he was free again. "Yeah," he said softly, looking down at her. "That's right—nothing to be afraid of."

He caught her up swiftly, tight and strong, feeling her soft mouth yield under his, and again he himself was gathered up in the warm dark, safe beyond sound or discovery, safe from being afraid, safe even from the dead.

When Danny walked through Main Street again that night toward his Aunt Jessie's house, he'd forgotten all about the little man in black who'd come to Bradford on the ten-ten. He noticed, without thinking anything about it, that the clock in the cupola above the courthouse said ten minutes to one. Down the street there was a little light falling across the sidewalk from the big front window of the Citizens' Bank, but that was usual. They always left a light on in the bank so the night policeman could see if prowlers were inside. But as Danny came closer the light across the sidewalk faded as if the current had weakened or someone had switched off a second light inside. A minute later he was at the window, looking in.

He saw that it must have been another light that had been switched off. Across the marble floor of the bank, beyond the partition that separated the cashier's and bookkeeper's space from the customers, Danny saw J. B. Sykes's broad back and head. J. B. was wearing a light coat and hat and he seemed to be talking to someone who must have been sitting at a desk maybe, out of sight behind the partition. While Danny watched, J. B. raised himself from the counter where he'd been leaning and moved toward the door. Another light switched off.

Standing in the darkness of the arched entrance to the bank, Danny heard two pairs of heels clicking across the marble floor inside. The door opened and the first to come out was the little man in black. His narrow face had a satisfied look as if he were proud of himself for working so late. He waited while J. B. locked the bank door and then they walked out on the sidewalk. For a minute they stood there not saying anything while J. B. stared glumly across the street and the little man waited politely. Still staring across the street, J. B. said something that Danny couldn't hear—but he heard the answer.

"We can't do business that way, Mr. Sykes," said the little man. "I know you're anxious, but being anxious won't fetch us all the answers we need to know. There's only one person who can give us all the answers."

"And what if you don't find him?" J. B. asked.

The little man's voice was bright and helpful. "We practically always do, Mr. Sykes," he said. "Not a hundred percent to be sure. But practically always." He held out his hand and J. B. took it without seeming to notice what he was doing. "At any rate, I'll be in first thing in the morning. Things always look better in the morning, I think, Mr. Sykes. Good night."

The little man tipped his hat and turned and walked toward the town hotel. Danny watched him go—little and skinny and black and carrying a briefcase like he'd been born with it in his hand. The little man had a brisk way of walking, almost cheerful, as if he were enjoying the night air.

Chapter Four

Friday it rained, and it wasn't until nearly a week later that Mose stopped by Aunt Jessie's to leave word that he was taking some lodge members hunting that night. Danny was gone at the time—more and more he was staying away from home, away from Bradford and Main Street and the people whose faces he'd seen, and who'd seen his, day after day, year after year. It had gotten so that everything they said seemed to hold some dark meaning to it, that when they looked at him there was a suspicion back of their eyes, that when he walked down Main Street they whispered behind his back. He left town early and didn't come back till after dark, in time to meet Gilly out at the culvert and walk out toward Blackwater—except those evenings when Gilly had to correct weekly test papers. The day of the hunt Danny had caught a ride over to Jamesburg ten miles away and stayed in a movie theater all day because he couldn't think of anything else to do. He came home just in time to get Mose's message and start out for the plantation.

Billy Scripture was already there when Danny came down the path behind the old mansion to Mose's shack. So were the lodge men, standing around in front of the shack waiting for Mose to fetch the hounds. Danny went past them and up the steps without saying anything. Mose was inside wrapping up a couple of bologna sandwiches. He put them inside his shirt with a pint of corn liquor before he and Danny went out to the pen to pick out the dogs. Mose picked eight—he didn't want to take Daisy Bell so soon after littering but she begged so hard that he let her out of the pen with the others. The hounds scattered down the path in the direction of the swamp right away. Mose and Danny and Billy Scripture followed and the lodge men fell in behind them.

They moved along in loose little groups for about twenty minutes, then struck off the path onto higher ground skirting the swamp. A late September moon was rising bright as a silver dollar, and gradually everything became as light as day, everything except little clumps of jack pine and the dark edge of the swamp itself. Sometimes way in the distance one of the dogs would give a yelp, but not a baying that meant anything. Mose just kept moving, with Danny and the men following, cutting through gullies and across stubble fields with little Negro shanties among the corn shocks, sending white wood smoke from the chimneys up against the shiny blue sky. Now and then in the damp bottoms they would wade hip-deep through ground fog, and when they got closer to the swamp they could see the white mist banked under the trees like snow.

After a while Mose changed his course again and began moving into the swamp. In the dark, men stumbled over broken trunks and swore against the branches that slashed their faces. They spread out more and more, each man taking his own way through the brush, until they kept together only by the sound of one another's voices. Danny moved slow and steady in the direction of the last dog's yelp, coming close to men, so close that he didn't see them until he heard them breathing. Once a match flared up suddenly over a pipe bowl, and Danny saw the face of one of the lodge men—just the face, nothing else, like a head hanging under the trees.

At last he found Mose with Billy, standing at the edge of a little clearing, listening for the dogs.

"Hear anything?" Danny asked.

"Not yet," said Mose. "Couple of minutes ago I heard one of them yelp. But nothing that meant anything."

"Aren't we bearing pretty much to the east?"

"Pretty much," said Mose.

"That's going to fetch us up right smack in Brothers Pond," Danny said. "Nothing but swamp between us and the pond."

Mose grinned a little and jerked his head back toward the lodge men still crashing around under the trees. "At least those fellows'll get their money's worth. Might even get their feet wet."

"Ain't no coon around Brothers Pond," Danny said.

Mose didn't answer. He'd stopped listening to Danny, was listening to something far away. Danny heard it too—a long yelp with a bell sound to it. A minute later it came again, then once more. Pretty soon the rest of the pack began joining in, baying the way they did when they hit a scent.

Mose spoke without turning his head. "Sounds like they got something. Which direction would you say?"

"A little to the north and east," Danny told him.

"Due east," said Mose. He looked at Danny and grinned. "Who says there's no coon at Brothers Pond?"

They began walking again, faster now, but the going was tougher, too. The brush got thicker and every now and then they'd hit little stagnant shallows of water where the tree roots stood above the ground like claws. The whole pack was in full cry now and the swamp echoed so bad that it was hard to keep direction. Danny figured they must be over a mile ahead and he stayed up front close to Mose trying to keep track of which way the pack was moving. As long as they kept bearing a little to the south they would lead to higher ground and he would be safe. But if they stuck to the bottom that stretched out right to the edge of Brothers Pond they might find a lot more than coon.

They must have been hurrying through the swamp for nearly an hour, trying to keep up with the dogs, when all of a sudden it seemed as if the whole pack had gone crazy and began yelping fast and all at once. Mose and Danny and Billy were together in a little patch of swamp grass and the ground sucked at their feet but they tried to move faster, tried to skirt the deep swamp to get to where the dogs were. Up ahead the yelping got more and more excited every minute. Finally they broke through the last brush and there high up in a tree sat Mister Coon, his bright button eyes looking straight into the beam of Mose's flashlight.

Danny got in among the dogs and started climbing the tree. Coon was sitting in a notch, his little head bent down, watching. As Danny came up the trunk coon left the notch and moved farther up the tree like a clumsy, furry beetle. Again he waited until Danny got close, then climbed out on a limb and turned, undecided between watching Danny and the hounds swarming and leaping over each other's backs down below. Danny braced himself against the trunk and, slowly, he began to shake the limb. Ten feet away, coon just dug in and held on. Again Danny shook the branch, but coon still wouldn't budge and down below Mose hollered, "Watch out, Daniel, you don't shake yourself out of the tree instead of coon!"

It was then that Danny began to get angry, blind angry—as if coon had a secret and was laughing at him, making fun of him. Danny began to talk to coon, cursing him in a voice low and full of hate as he moved out along the branch, trying to reach coon with his bare fist and knock him off. But again coon inched out on the branch, until the tip began to give under his weight. Once more Danny began to heave his whole weight up and down. Around the bottom of the tree the dogs stopped yelping for half a second, their bodies crouched and quivering, waiting for coon to fall. Then suddenly one of coon's hind legs lost its grip, and before coon could get his balance Danny gave the branch another shake and coon went down.

For a minute Danny just lay on the limb too tired to move, too tired even to figure why he'd gotten so mad at poor old coon. A second later he knew—coon had brought the hunt to the last place on earth that Danny wanted to see. Down through the tops of the other trees there was moonlight shining on Brothers Pond.

When Danny came down, coon was in Mose's burlap bag and the dogs had quieted down a little. The lodge men were sitting under the trees, talking among themselves and passing around a bottle. Mose was sitting apart with Billy Scripture. He reached into his shirt for the paper sack with the bologna sandwiches. He gave one to Billy and offered the other one to Danny.

"I'm not hungry," Danny said. "Let's start back."

"Here, take a drink."

"I don't want a drink."

"Then sit down," said Mose. "Got to rest before we start all that walking."

One of the men under the trees suddenly hollered, "Hey, Mose, what time is it?"

Mose looked at his watch and called back, "Near four o'clock."

"Aren't we down near the pond somewhere?"

"That's right," said Mose. "Shouldn't be more than a quarter of a mile."

"Well, heck," said the man in the dark, "why don't we go over to the dance hall? There's a road from there to the highway."

"Ain't going to catch a ride at this hour," Danny said.

"Anyway, walking's easier," said the man.

Daisy Bell came out of the brush about then and stuck her nose in Mose's lap. Mose shoved her away but she came back, whining through her nose.

"Something wrong with your dog? She get hurt?" asked a man who'd walked over from the others.

Mose held Daisy Bell quiet while he looked to see if the coon had hurt her. But she broke away after a minute and ran off among the other dogs moving around in the dark, their noses to the ground.

"What's eating them dogs?" Mose said. "They're restless."

"Scent-crazy," Danny said.

"Don't make a noise like that for coon," Mose answered slowly. "Maybe somebody else off in the woods."

Danny laughed, short and nervous. "Who's going to prowl around the swamp this time of night?"

Mose didn't answer. He took another drink of corn, threw the bottle away, and stood up. "Tell those fellows to come along," he said. "We'll be lucky if we get back to town by daylight."

"Ain't we going back same as we come?" Danny asked.

"Why?" Mose said. "Save three miles on the road and it's easier. Besides, some of those fellows look like they want to be carried back."

Danny didn't say any more and when Mose struck off toward the pond he fell in behind him. Billy and the lodge men straggled along in the back and the hounds were prowling all over, crashing off into the brush and then ducking out again right under a man's legs. Sometimes they made little worried sounds high in their throats.

"Don't know what's belly-aching those dogs," said Mose.

"There's a path comes around on this side of the pond somewhere," said one of the men, "where all the fellers bring the girls between dances to show them the view."

"We're practically on the path right now," said Mose.

A minute later they were on it. The dogs were running back and forth on the path as nervous as a bitch who's lost her pups. They kept sniffing loudly and Danny began to watch them, afraid they'd come near him. "They've found something, sure as sin," said Mose. He sounded serious. It was as if everybody—or at least that was the way it seemed to Danny—had begun to feel that something was wrong, that the dogs were trying to tell them something and that it was just a matter of time before somebody caught on. Danny wanted to run and hide in the bushes, just run and disappear and never come back, to Bradford or Main Street or Aunt Jessie's house.

But he knew that was the one thing he shouldn't do—run. So he stayed close to Mose, watching Mose's back and hoping that Mose wouldn't hear his heart pounding. It was so heavy and loud that the weight of it made him feel sick inside. Already he could see bushes that looked like they'd been broken, already they were at the place where they'd done most of the fighting. And then, just ahead, Danny heard a long, lonely howl—almost a wail. When they came around the bend they saw the dog, sitting in the middle of the path, back on his haunches, nose pointed at the moon. The other dogs had disappeared, but Danny could hear them, whining and moaning, off to the right toward the pond.

Mose didn't say anything, just turned on his flashlight and moved off the path toward the water's edge. Danny stepped off the path too, then waited. Off in the brush he could see Mose's flashlight beam swinging from side to side. Then it stopped swinging and held steady.

Couple of minutes later he heard Mose move again. The flashlight clicked off and Mose came back through the brush to where Danny was standing. Some of the lodge men had caught up by now and were crowding around, seeing by Mose's face that something was wrong. "Anything the matter?" asked the man Danny had seen light his pipe in the swamp. But Mose just stood there without answering and the men went down and found out for themselves. Danny could hear one of them being sick.

"Why don't you talk?" Danny asked after a while. It was like it hurt him to talk too.

Mose moved as if he'd just started thinking again. "Got to get back to town," he said, his voice deep. "There's a man down there—" he waited before he said it—"dead."

"Who is it?"

"Can't very well tell," Mose said. "But haven't they been looking for Jerry Sykes?"

At Danny's feet something furry brushed against his leg and whined. "Get away—damn you!" Danny said. Before he knew what he was doing he raised his foot and kicked, kicked hard as he could. Daisy Bell bounced off into the brush, squealing and yelping.

He heard Mose's voice again. "Ain't no reason to kick the dog— she didn't kill Jerry Sykes."

Danny raised his head sharply to see what the Negro meant by that. But Mose's face didn't tell him anything. It was just tired and heavy and sad.

"Let's get going," said Mose.

It was only after they'd started moving toward the main road, everybody quiet, that Danny realized Billy Scripture wasn't next to him. He fell back to the end of the line, just in time to see Billy hurrying up the path trying to catch up with the others. "Stick around, Billy," Danny said, a little angry, "or you'll get lost." He let Billy go past him and then followed. Billy couldn't make his feet move very fast, but somehow he managed to keep up. As he shuffled along he kept his right hand in his pocket, almost as if he were afraid of losing something. But Danny didn't think anything of it. Only later—not at the time.

Chapter Five

Judd Jenkins was sweeping out his hardware store when Danny came in. He threw a couple of handfuls of wet sawdust across the wooden floor, then took a broom to it. Danny watched him, thinking of what he was going to pretend to buy.

"Keeps the dust down," said Judd, poking the broom along a row of nail kegs. "Danged stuff gets in the air and first thing I know I got the asthma. Can't hardly breathe. You in a hurry for something?"

"You got a gig?"

"A gig? Going frog hunting, eh?" Judd went on sweeping. "Thought you was going to ask for nails. Wouldn't believe it but them folks down at the fairgrounds just about cleaned me out of everything— three-penny, five-penny, ten-penny, all sizes. Must be a powerful bull when you got to hammer his pen with ten-penny nails. What was it you wanted?"

"A gig, if you got one."

"You been down there yet?"

"Where?"

"The fairgrounds."

"No."

"Haven't, eh?" Judd shook his head. "Something I noticed. Folks don't give much of a dang no more about county fairs. It was different years ago. Farmers'd send in stock from fifty miles away. Opening Day there'd be six brass bands playing all at onct and parades and high-wire performers. I wrestled a bear one year, a genuine cinnamon bear. Don't mind while I finish sweeping?"

Danny was getting restless. Judd liked to talk his customers to death, hated to see them go. Folks said a man had gone in one morning to buy five cents' worth of staples and when he got home he was late for supper. "Listen," said Danny, "I don't care if you ain't got the shaft for the gig. If you got the barb I can make my own shaft."

"Well, we'll have to see. I don't know what I got in that back room."

Across the room was the single glass showcase. Danny tried to keep from looking at it while Judd was around, but he knew what was in it—magnifying glasses, flashlights, cigarette lighters, knives....

"Ain't seen the deaf boy, have you?" Judd was saying. "He made out of here yesterday with the reflector off a flashlight worth seventy-nine cents."

"Billy don't mean nothing."

"I know he don't mean nothing. All the same the flashlight was worth seventy-nine cents." Judd set his broom in the corner behind the counter. For a minute he stared through the window crammed with rakes and saws and fire extinguishers and hose. It was still early and not many people about. Across the street an old Negro woman was washing the courthouse steps.

"Sure you want the gig now?" asked Judd again. "I might have to climb up a stepladder and I don't want to break my leg for nothing."

"If you got one I want it."

As soon as Judd had gone into the back room, Danny crossed over to the glass case and bent over it. There were all sorts of knives in the trays—penknives, jack-knives, Boy Scout knives, and hunting knives with pressed leather or bone handles—but he saw only one, the one he was afraid might have been sold. It had a shaggy deer hide handle, a five-inch spring blade, exactly like the knife he had lost. It had a price tag on it: six eighty-five. Judd would remember if he missed something that cost as much as that. But maybe nobody would buy a knife for days. By that time anybody could have stolen the knife.

Just then a little bell rang and Danny turned in time to see Sheriff Otis close the door behind him. He didn't say anything to Danny, not even good morning, as if he were too busy thinking to notice anybody. He prowled around for a few minutes while Danny sweated and waited, thinking he'd lost the chance to take the knife. He heard Clem go out to the back room looking for Judd. Slowly Danny inched back the glass top on the case and reached for the knife. He had just lifted it out of the case, still hadn't moved back the glass top, when Judd's voice made him jump. "That's a danged good knife, Daniel."

"I was just looking."

"I'll make you a price on it."

Danny heard Clem walking back toward them along the counter. All of a sudden he had a feeling that he was trapped, that Judd was going to talk him into admitting that he'd killed Jerry Sykes—and all of it in front of Clem. He got rattled and figured the best way was to go through with the sale.

"How much you want for it?"

"Well, lemme see," said Judd, reading the price tag. He figured in his mind for a minute before he said, "Let you have it for five dollars. Couldn't make a better buy than that, could you, Sheriff?"

Clem reached over and took the knife from Judd, opened the blade, and ran his thumb along the edge. "I don't know," he said, handing the knife back to Judd, and talking as if he weren't much interested either way. "I don't know anything about the price of knives."

"Well, at five dollars she's a bargain, take my word for it," said Judd. "Only reason I'm making the offer is nobody wants this type of knife. Only had two and this is one of them. Sold the other one last spring to a young feller—" Judd suddenly stopped and opened his eyes. "Why heck, it was you," he said to Danny. "Why you need another one?"

"I lost mine," Danny said, and right away he wished he could have put the words back in his mouth. It was the wrong thing to say and he knew it. Everything had been a mistake—even trying to steal the knife in the first place. But he hadn't figured on getting caught, on Clem coming in, or on getting rattled.

It was then he realized something else too. Judd and Clem were staring through the window full of rakes toward the street, not saying anything. The coroner's car, the one with the black enclosed rear body, had pulled up in front of the courthouse steps, and while Danny and Judd and Clem watched, the coroner and his assistant got out and went to the back and opened the double rear door. The assistant climbed inside and the two men lifted a stretcher from the car. On the stretcher was something wrapped in canvas and tied down with ropes at both ends.

"God a-mighty," Judd said in a low voice. "There been another wreck somewheres?"

"Murder's more like it," said Clem. "That's what's left of Sykes's boy."

"God a-mighty," Judd whispered. "God a-mighty."

Danny heard his feet walk across the wooden floor, the leather heels clomping across the boards as if they were made of lead. He wondered if Judd was going to remember that he was leaving without buying the knife. But Judd must have forgotten because Danny reached the door without being called back. He opened the door and closed it, hearing the little bell ring both times, way off as if it were back in his own mind somewhere and hurt. Then he was standing in the glare of the sunshine outside. The door of Jenkins' Hardware opened again, making the little bell ring.

"Daniel," he heard Sheriff Otis say.

Danny didn't even look around—he just slowed down until he felt Clem's hand on his shoulder as Clem came alongside him. "Which way you walking, boy?" Clem asked.

"Nowhere particular."

"Well then, I'll walk you a piece," said Clem. They crossed the street to the courthouse side and went down the block together. But the sheriff didn't say anything. He just kept chewing the stub of a cigar as if he were thinking. Danny walked slow beside him, hoping he'd be able to talk natural when Clem started asking questions, but right then he wasn't even sure he could talk out loud—his throat had suddenly gone so dry it hurt him to swallow.

"I been wanting to talk to you, Daniel," the sheriff began finally in his slow kind of way. "Especially since what you fellers found last night at Brothers Pond. Tell me—you were down at that last dance they had at Brothers Landing before they closed for the season?"

"That's right," Danny said. "That's the night I piled up Jimmy Biff's sedan."

"Been drinking, hadn't you?"

"A little."

"Quite a lot, the way I heard it."

"It was the rain. I couldn't see the road."

"Not when you're moving at sixty-three miles an hour."

"It wasn't that fast."

"That's what the speedometer said when I saw the car next day. Somebody must have put salt in your breeches to make you want to run that fast," said the sheriff. He threw away the chewed cigar stub. "Anyway, that ain't what I wanted to talk about. I wanted to ask you about the dance."

"What you want to know?"

"Did you see Jerry Sykes while you were at the dance?"

"I saw him."

"What was he doing at the time?"

"He was dancing with Gilly Johnson."

"Isn't that the schoolteacher you drove home that night, the one in the wreck with you?"

"That's right."

"You took her to the dance?"

"No. I think Jerry brought her."

"If Jerry brought her, how come you took her home?"

"Jerry wasn't around."

"You sweet on this Gilly Johnson, by any chance?"

That was a dangerous question and Danny knew it. You couldn't answer maybe, you had to say yes or no. Danny didn't wait. "No," he said.

"Uh-huh," Sheriff Otis said as if the question hadn't meant much one way or the other. "When Jerry and the schoolteacher were dancing, what time would you say it was?"

"I don't know."

"Just approximate."

"Oh, maybe anywhere from ten to eleven-thirty. They danced together a lot."

The sheriff gave a sour little grunt. "I haven't heard anybody yet that agreed on the time. Jerry could have left the floor anywhere from ten to one-thirty. You didn't see him go, did you?"

"No."

"Were you inside all evening?"

"I went out once to the car around eleven o'clock. I got a drink from Jimmy Biff."

The sheriff seemed to pass over that. "You didn't notice if Jerry had words with anybody—an argument or something?"

"No."

Clem stopped for a minute and bit the end off a fresh Garcia Grande. "Know of anybody had a grudge against Jerry?"

"Lots of folks didn't like Jerry."

"Yes, I know," Clem said. "But I mean particular. Like you, for instance."

"Why should I have a grudge against Jerry?"

"Didn't he devil you a lot about your father?"

"Some."

"And I hear Jerry tarred you one night."

"That was when we were kids. I ain't got that long a memory."

Clem looked at Danny kind of sharp for a minute. "They tell me you were always a little different from the others at school—kind of kept off to yourself. Sensitive, they called it."

"You got a lot of information, looks like."

"Just asking around," said Sheriff Otis. "Course, feller like you— I don't blame you for being sensitive. I never knew too much about your father's case, but it ain't fair his son should have to live under the cloud of it, no matter how bad it was."

"Pa didn't do any more than any ordinary man would have done with his reasons. That's what the lawyer said."

"I ain't arguing your father's case, Daniel," said the sheriff kind of gentle. "'Pears it's a mite late for that. What I'm driving at is a lot closer than that. I got a boy lying on a slab in the coroner's office—murdered. And I got to get to the truth of it. A man's been murdered, somebody had to do it. And whoever did it had to have reasons. Sometimes you got facts and you get the reasons later. But when you ain't got facts you look for reasons that'll lead you to the facts."

"And what if you don't get the facts?" Danny asked, trying to make the question sound easy, not too interested.

"Then you don't convict," said Clem. "Shucks, I know half a dozen thieves in this county, know they stole just as sure as I'm standing here, but I ain't got the facts to hang it on them." Clem stood on the sidewalk for a minute, looking at the end of his cigar. "Maybe," he said, "nobody will ever find out who left Jerry Sykes's body in the water at Brothers Pond. But it's a funny thing, Daniel. A small town is like a stomach, always digestin'. Eat a green apple, nothing happens right away, but two hours later you get a bellyache. Take Bradford here. Something can happen maybe in the middle of the night with all the curtains down—and the town don't take much notice, just goes along looking quiet and peaceful like she does right now. But folks talk, Danny, and sometimes the talk adds up after a while and hell breaks loose. Shucks, I can catch me a criminal quicker just going along Main Street and listening than I can with a pack of bloodhounds."

Danny didn't say anything. He stood there thinking while Clem rolled the cigar gloomily between his fingers, thinking of the half-dozen thieves who'd never been caught, thinking of what Clem had said about the town talking and how it added up sometimes. That was what he never could figure—what people were saying behind his back. He couldn't even figure always when he had said something wrong, something that might kick back on him later. And he went back over what the sheriff had asked, wondering if he'd made a slip somewhere—a little slip that the sheriff had let pass but ticked off in a ledger somewhere in his mind waiting for other slips, other bits of talk, waiting to add up the sum.

The sheriff was asking him a question again. "Ever gamble any, Daniel?"

"Not much. Craps sometimes."

"I mean the card games that went on down at Brothers Pond in the back room. They tell me the pots get pretty big sometimes. Over seven hundred dollars one night."

"I ain't got that kind of money."

"No, guess you haven't. Neither have I," said the sheriff. "But what about that Williams boy, the one that leads the band. He scatters quite a bit of money around."

"What you mean—what about him?"

"You didn't notice if he left the stand any time during the evening?"

"Sure he left the stand. There's ten-minute breaks between dances." Danny felt an excitement gathering in him and he had to hold it down. He was answering Clem's questions too fast.

"What I mean is—did he ever seem upset or seem to have anything on his mind?"

"Why don't you ask him?" Danny asked.

"Uh-huh." The sheriff puffed at his cigar without saying any more. Then he threw it away, half smoked. "Well, I got to go back to the courthouse now. I appreciate talking to you, Danny."

"That's all right, Sheriff. Glad to help." Danny watched Clem's stooped shoulders and the loose-fitting clothes as the sheriff moved down the sidewalk and on toward the side entrance of the courthouse. He felt like he'd just won a victory or something like it. Clem couldn't have thought Danny did it or he wouldn't have asked those last questions about Ken Williams.

Danny felt lighter, as if something had been lifted from him, as if he had awakened from some terrible dream just at the last moment. Around him the street was suddenly alive with people, he heard sounds, felt the sun warm on his skin. It was as if he had been numb for a long time and now suddenly seeing and hearing and smelling and feeling had come back into his body. He started walking, back toward Aunt Jessie's. But he hadn't walked six steps before he stopped again and his heart started to pound.

Directly ahead of him, across the street, was Amos Green's used car agency, and in the main show window stood the shiny red roadster, Jerry Sykes's Buick.

When Danny jerked his head to look back, Clem had already disappeared into the courthouse. Maybe he was already at some window inside, watching to see how Danny acted when he saw Jerry's car. Had the sheriff walked him here on purpose or was he just imagining things? Danny didn't know the answer. But when he began walking again, more slowly now, he no longer heard the sounds of Main Street, no longer felt the sun.

By the time Danny got back to Aunt Jessie's it was nearly noon. When he opened the front door he could smell cooking, but it sickened him and he went straight upstairs to his own room and lay down on the bed. He hadn't been sleeping much at night and he felt tired. For a long time he lay there without moving, listening to Aunt Jessie bustle around in the kitchen. After a while he could hear her footsteps on the stair, then a light knock on his door and Aunt Jessie asking if he was ready for lunch. Danny told her he'd already eaten at Billy's Drug. There was a short silence before he heard her footsteps going back down the stairs.

He must have gone to sleep after that because when he opened his eyes a late afternoon sun was already slanting into the room. Through the floor grill that let heat circulate through the house he heard women's voices in the sitting room below. Judging by the amount of talk and the rattle of the tea cups there must have been near a dozen women in the sitting room, and it took Danny a minute before he could figure that it must have been Aunt Jessie's turn to entertain the weekly meeting of the Ladies' Aid Society at her house. Most of the voices were just voices, but one or two Danny recognized—Clem Otis's wife, Judd Jenkins' wife, Lydia Simpkins, who had never been anybody's wife, and Angela Peabody, whose husband was the oldest doctor in town.

At first Danny couldn't make sense out of the talk, and then Sarah Jenkins said something that made him get up out of bed and stand near the floor grill to hear better. "All the same," Sarah was saying, "all the same, think the town has got a right to know all the facts. I know it's natural for a father to want to save his son's good name, especially when he's—dead." Sarah slowed up on the word. "But after all, whose money is it that's in the bank if it isn't the town's?"

"J. B. Sykes is a lot more interested in saving his own face than his son's, dead or alive." Angela Peabody had a voice almost like a man's and she said things straight out in a way that shocked people.

"Well, it's like I told Judd," Sarah said quickly before anybody else could cut in. "If you can't even trust your own banker's son not to take money out of the cash box, who can you trust? I told Judd to take every cent out of the Citizens' Bank this afternoon and take it to Jamesburg or put it in a sock, anywhere but just get it out of the Citizens' Bank."

"Maybe the boy didn't really mean to take so much." Aunt Jessie's voice was sad, like it was a personal sorrow. "Maybe he was just led astray."

"Humph," said Lydia Simpkins. "Nobody ever led Jerry Sykes Junior astray. Maybe the other way around, but never Jerry. This isn't the first time that his father has had to get him out of some mess or other."

"But it's the last, apparently," said Angela Peabody, making a joke that was either too grim or else nobody understood because nobody laughed. "How much did the boy take when all's said and done?"

"Way over two thousand dollars—at least that's the way I heard it," said Sarah Jenkins. "Old J. B. tried to get the bank examiner to keep the whole thing quiet and just let him make up the amount out of his own pocket. But I guess J. B. didn't impress him any. He just put his foot down and said no."

"Strange little man, that Mr. Updyke," said Angela Peabody. "He's come and gone with a nod and a smile—and nobody any the wiser until today. When I saw him in church Sunday I thought he'd come to bury somebody."

"I think he looked fine," Sarah Jenkins answered. "I been trying to get Judd to wear a black suit to church for years. I think a black suit in church looks nice. It shows respect."

"Nonsense!" said Angela. "Judd Jenkins can come to church in a fig leaf for all I care as long as he's got heaven on his mind."

"Angela Peabody!"

Sarah was so shocked that Aunt Jessie broke in to smooth things over. "I think that Angela just meant that it isn't what you wear, it's what you think when you go to church that matters."

There was silence until Clem Otis's wife broke in for the first time. "Anybody going down to the fair tonight?"

"Heavens, yes," said Sarah Jenkins. "And I wish I wasn't. I'll be a cripple for days afterward. But I can't keep Judd away. I think if I let him go he'd just follow one of those carnival things for the rest of his life. He can't forget he wrestled a cinnamon bear forty years back."

"Maybe I could ride in your car?" asked Clem's wife. "I've got a can of pickled beets and a jar of marmalade up for the blue ribbon."

"Well, you come right along with us," said Sarah, "and we'll be happy to have you. Why can't the sheriff go—his lumbago on him again?"

"No. I think the sheriff"—Clem's wife always spoke of him as the sheriff in public—"is going to be busy tonight."

"You got something on your mind, Martha," Angela Peabody's voice broke in again. "You haven't opened your mouth all afternoon. For you that isn't natural."

"Well, I haven't opened it on purpose," answered Martha Otis and her voice sounded kind of peevish. "I figured it was better for the news to come out natural."

"What news, Martha?" asked Sarah Jenkins sharply. "Has the sheriff made an arrest yet?" Her voice dropped almost to a whisper that Danny couldn't hear.

"Well, not exactly —"

"Stop spinning it out, Martha," said Angela Peabody. "You were waiting all afternoon for the best time to break the news. Now let's have it."

"Well, the sheriff did take a man into custody this afternoon, just before I got here. Just for questioning though, he said."

Right away everybody began asking questions, and Danny lost track of who was asking them. Finally Martha Otis said, "If you'd all stop asking questions I'll tell you. It's the Williams boy, the one that leads the band."

Everybody seemed to say "Poor Mrs. Williams," at the same time, in low, hushed voices, and then Sarah Jenkins broke in again, "What made him do it?"

"He ain't convicted yet, Sarah," Angela Peabody reminded her.

"Well, if Sheriff Otis takes a man in for questioning, I know he's almost a hundred per cent sure already that he did it."

"What makes the sheriff think Ken Williams is guilty?" Angela Peabody asked Clem's wife.

"Well, that's why Jerry was taking all the money from the bank. He owed it to the Williams boy and he wasn't paying fast enough."

"How could he owe money to the Williams boy?"

"Gambling."

"Gambling?"

"Down at Brothers Pond."

Upstairs in his room Danny didn't hear any more. He didn't need to. At first the talk had led him deeper and deeper into some sickening darkness in which he half expected the sheriff's hand to touch his shoulder again as it had that morning. But now he was breathing again, breathing deep and with every breath it seemed as if some wild kind of freedom were returning to him. He wanted suddenly to find Gilly, to touch her and maybe for the first time laugh with her. He went to the closet and took out his best suit and laid it on the bed. Then he went into the bathroom to wash.

Downstairs the talk went on. Lydia Simpkins was speaking her piece. "I'm not a bit surprised," she said. "Many's the time I've gone to the Christian Endeavor of a Sunday night and wondered how many of those young people had been at Brothers Pond dancing the night before. If I'd had my way, the town would have closed that dance hall right after it opened. I'd like to know what God thinks about it."

"I don't think God's been in the habit of speaking his mind to ordinary common human beings," said Angela Peabody, "much less the Ladies' Aid Society."

"Well, he spoke it in the Bible—no guess work there."

"I think it's mighty easy for us to sit here and say the younger generation's going to perdition," said Aunt Jessie quietly. "But maybe it ain't their fault, maybe it's ours. We don't bring them up right, we don't teach them right."

"You just said something, Jessie," Lydia Simpkins answered. "And I think it's about time we began checking on the kind of schoolteachers we've got in Bradford."

"Like whom?" asked Angela Peabody.

"Like that young Gilly Johnson, for instance. Entirely too lively for my taste."

"She's a good, intelligent, conscientious girl," said Angela. "And I've never heard a bad word spoken of her—except about the wreck and from what I hear that wasn't her fault."

"I'm not just talking about the wreck," said Lydia Simpkins.

"Well, what are you complaining about?"

"Everybody knows that she and Jerry Sykes had been going together—fixing to get married, it looked like to me. Wouldn't you say it was kind of strange if overnight she began mooning over the fence with somebody entirely different?"

"Who?" asked Sarah Jenkins.

"I think I've done enough talking for one afternoon."

"I think you have," said Angela.

"Tell us," said Sarah.

"I wouldn't want to hurt Jessie's feelings."

"How could you hurt my feelings?" asked Aunt Jessie, surprised.

"Well, that boy I'm talking about—I wouldn't have to throw a stone very far to where he lives."

"You mean Daniel?" asked Aunt Jessie.

"Daniel Hawkins," said Lydia Simpkins.

"Sh-h," somebody put a finger to her lips. "I think he's coming down the stairs. You wouldn't want to embarrass the boy."

For a minute nobody said anything and there was only the rattle of the tea cups. The front door slammed shut and Sarah Jenkins got up and wiped the cake crumbs off her bosom.

"Well, well—that's a lot of news for one afternoon," she said. "Would anybody else like to come to the fair?"

Chapter Six

It wasn't until they got out past Main and Poplar that Danny and Gilly could see the fairgrounds, the big tan-colored tents, the pennants and the lights, the Ferris wheel turning against the night. There were cars from all over the county and as far away as Candy Ridge, all parked along both shoulders of the road and even in any pasture they could drive into. And on the road itself, dodging cars, were the people coming and going to the fair, farmers and gangs of boys, old ladies with chokers and kids with balloons and yellow canaries on sticks. At the gate that led into the sawdust-covered midway there was a crush of people, and Danny had to wait for nearly half an hour just to get the tickets.

He was glad that it was crowded, that he could belong and be a part of the crowd, and standing in the long line before the ticket window while Gilly looked around the nearby booths, Danny thought to himself: I'm just like anybody else in this line waiting to put money on the counter. I'll put down the same kind of money and get the same kind of tickets. All his life he'd felt like he was different, on the outside—and now the feeling had stopped. Ever since they'd found Jerry Sykes's body, Danny had had a tight feeling in his back as if at any moment somebody was going to step up behind him and say, "Come along, Daniel." But the women's talk at Aunt Jessie's had changed that, and in a queer kind of way he didn't feel any kind of responsibility toward Ken Williams. He thought of Ken as something apart from the killing, as if it were Ken's own fault that circumstances said he'd committed the killing. If Ken had gambled with Jerry and it put the finger on him—well, that was his bad luck and he'd been caught for it.

The important thing was that Danny was in the clear, that he felt free again, free to mix with other people, free to act like other people, without being afraid that they were talking about him because he knew now that they were talking about somebody else, about Ken Williams. What was it Mose had said about animals acting guilty? You acted guilty and pretty soon people began thinking you were guilty, you thought people were watching you kind of odd and pretty soon they really were, you were afraid that you were going to act in a way that was different from normal and pretty soon, just because that was the thing you were most afraid of, you did begin acting queer. It was a strange thing, Danny thought, that a man who knows something about himself and is afraid begins to show it in spite of himself. But now he didn't have to act guilty because he wasn't afraid anymore.

Even Gilly had noticed when he met her that a change had come over him. "You want to go to the fair?" she asked, looking at him curiously in the dark. "All those people?"

"Why not?" asked Danny. "Can't keep this a secret forever."

"Yes, I know," Gilly had answered slowly. "It's just hard to understand, I guess." She gave a little shrug with her shoulders. "It's like we've been meeting in the dark so much it's a habit. I'd never thought what it might be like just to walk down Main Street with you. Why should I be afraid? Why should I have been afraid all this time?"

"No reason," said Danny. "No reason at all."

And yet as they walked among the side shows and the exhibit buildings, where every housewife in Bradford County had sent at least a jar of pickles or canned peaches for the blue ribbon, Danny listened to the shouting of the barkers and the distant banging of carnival music and began to feel something else. Something like he'd felt the Saturday night of the killing—a feeling that all this crowd and noise and music and lights wasn't real, like it was something you saw and heard in a fever maybe. And behind it that other feeling, the dangerous feeling, of not even wanting to be safe the way he thought. It was like that music pounding over and over in the distance was the blood in his body pounding—a thing saying he was different, better, that he was a winner and wanted to prove it. It was like when he'd been driving Jimmy Biff's sedan and couldn't take his foot off the accelerator.

Gilly was holding onto his arm as they walked through the crowd that jostled and bumped into them. Now and then they stopped to look at the booths or to listen to a sideshow barker. Danny wondered where they'd all come from—the dark man and the woman in the gypsy skirt, who seemed to lie rigid in mid-air when the dark man waved his hands; a man with one foot in a sling, standing against the side of a bending pole seventy-five feet above the midway; a dancer beating a tambourine as she whirled on a platform; the tattooed lady with a boa constrictor curled around her neck; fire-swallowers, fortunetellers, and freaks. Up and down the midway people walking and gawking, eating boxes of crackerjacks, candied red apples. And above the sound of the crowd, above the squawking of noisemakers, the hollering of the hawkers, and the occasional bellow of a bull at the livestock exhibit, came the over-and-over clanging of a calliope.

So far nobody had recognized them, nobody had even said hello. It was as if being part of the crowd had given him a disguise, and Danny had a sudden, wonderful feeling that this was what the world was like, a world where everybody wore a disguise. Everybody, it seemed like, was something else than what they looked like— liars, beggars, clowns, thieves, murderers, freaks. Everybody was guilty of something, and because of that nobody was more guilty than anyone else. Mose was wrong. Men didn't always look guilty....

"Buy me a spun sugar." Danny felt Gilly tug at his arm and turned and smiled. She was smiling too, but her face turned serious while he looked at her.

"Gilly ..." he said softly.

"What is it, Daniel?"

"Just Gilly," he repeated. "It's a nice name and I'm glad we came."

She pressed his arm. "I'm glad too. It's strange I should feel as happy as I do. And yet I've a feeling that—" Gilly broke off.

"You've got a feeling what?"

"Buy me a spun sugar," she said.

They went to the booth and waited while a man in a dirty apron caught the white stuff like cotton on a stick from a big turning basin. They walked through the crowd again. "You got a feeling what?" Danny asked again. He didn't like to leave sentences unfinished. They might be important.

"I don't want to talk about it," said Gilly. "It isn't often we've had an evening like this—not even often, never. I don't want to spoil it."

"You were going to say something before," Danny said. "I want you to finish it."

"It's just that I've got a feeling that I haven't a right being happy like this, with you," Gilly said slowly. They were both silent while Danny tried to figure what she meant. Then Gilly said, "You were right about Jerry Sykes, Danny. I never loved him."

"Yeah," said Danny. His voice sounded harder than he meant it. "When did you find this out?"

"Today," Gilly said. "When I heard it. Heard about what happened to Jerry. It was almost as if I'd read it in the papers and it had happened to somebody in another city, in another state, somebody whose name I'd hardly heard before. I felt sorry for Jerry like you feel sorry for anything bad that's happened."

"Ain't no use feeling sorry for Jerry. He's dead."

"I don't think anybody really feels sorry for Jerry," Gilly said. "Nobody liked him, but maybe nobody ever understood him either."

"I don't like talking about Jerry," said Danny.

"I know." Gilly turned and put her hand on Danny's arm again and pressed it. She looked up into his face as if she were trying to find an answer there to a question she was asking herself. "Only I keep wondering," she said, "who could have hated Jerry enough to kill him?"

"Maybe Jerry asked for it," Danny said. "Anyway, why put the question to me?"

Gilly shrugged her shoulders. "No reason—except that's what they asked me."

"Who?"

"The sheriff. What's his name? Clem Otis?"

They were standing in the glare of a booth and behind the counter a man was yelling, yelling without making any sound that Danny could hear. He was piling up mounds of baseballs on the counter and Danny asked himself in an odd sort of way—why should a man be piling up baseballs like that? Behind the man, ducks on an endless belt appeared, traveled quickly across a painted backdrop of marsh, and disappeared. And on the side walls on shelves, rows of kewpie dolls and rag dolls, boxes of candy tied with red silk ribbons. It didn't add up, it didn't make sense. What did baseballs have to do with ducks?

"Clem's been asking a lot of questions," Danny said. "What kind of questions?"

"Only what happened at Brothers Pond, how long I'd gone with Jerry, whether he'd had any arguments—"

"He must have asked about people. Who?"

"Ken Williams mostly. But he asked about everybody, even you. Asked if you'd ever showed a grudge against Jerry."

"What'd you tell him?"

"That I didn't know you that well." Gilly looked at him again and said as if she were realizing it for the first time. "That's true—I don't. Did you have a grudge against Jerry?"

"If you please, folks—" Danny heard the gravel-voiced man behind the counter. It reminded him of another voice, but where? Then suddenly he remembered—the night at Roy's, the drunken woman with the gray bangs, the hand on his wrist, the spot of blood on his cuff.

"If you please, folks," the man was saying, "either step up and take a chance or don't block the area for them as would like to. You got a good arm, young fellow. Why not take a chance and win the young lady a prize? Six balls for a quarter. Six balls to knock down the moving ducks. Three hits wins a box of candy, four hits a rag doll, and five a genuine kewpie doll for the mantelpiece. There you are, young fellow, six balls in a rack!"

Danny picked up the first ball, felt his fingers tighten on it and let go, watched a duck drop out of line. "One down, five to go!" cried the gravel-voiced man. Again Danny picked up a ball and watched another duck disappear.

"Baseball player, eh?" asked the man behind the counter. He began to cry out to the passing crowd. "Step right up, folks, and take a chance on the moving ducks. Watch the young man prove how easy it is to do it! Step right up. Six balls for a quarter! You there, what d'you say? What's the matter—can't you talk?"

Danny had the fifth ball in his fingers, let it go, heard the ball smack against the canvas backdrop as he turned. Down the counter stood Billy Scripture watching him, watching, it seemed to Danny, in the steady kind of way that a man has when he knows something about you.

"One more ball," said the man behind the counter.

"Keep it," Danny said without looking at him.

"Wait a minute, here's your prize!" the man cried loudly for the crowd to hear. Danny saw a rag doll shoved at Gilly across the counter, a rag doll with red checked pants, blue jacket, and white scarf.

"What am I going to do with this?" Gilly asked.

"You heard the man," said Danny. "Put it on your mantelpiece."

Down the counter Billy still didn't smile. Beside him, Danny heard Gilly say, "I don't have a mantelpiece—" She stopped short and her voice was different when she said, "That's what Jerry was wearing—"

"What?"

"White scarf, blue jacket—" Gilly suddenly looked up. "Daniel, I don't want this doll!"

Billy was coming toward them. But Billy wasn't looking at Danny, he was looking at the doll, looking at it the way a kid does.

"He wants the doll," Gilly said. "He can't take his eyes off it."

"Give it to him," said Danny. Gilly handed the dead stuffed thing to Billy. Danny took her arm and began guiding her through the crowd.

"Daniel, what's the matter? You're pushing people!"

"Let's get onto a ride." He was leading Gilly to the Ferris wheel, its string of lights circling in the dark, the gondolas swinging gently as the wheel turned. He bought tickets at the booth and handed them to the brakeman when he stopped the wheel and helped them into a gondola. The man pulled the brake again and they were rising, rising into the night.

Gilly was quiet at first, and when he reached out his hand to touch hers she didn't answer right away. "You're angry," she said quietly. "Why are you always angry so suddenly, Daniel?"

"I wasn't angry," he lied. "Look up. It's like you're floating." The wheel was at the top, circling over, and moving down toward the tents and the pennants and the little figures of people standing around the bottom. A kid lost a balloon in the gondola just ahead, and it floated yellow up into the night, the reflected light of the midway making it shine like a little moon until it disappeared. Somewhere, at the carrousel with its frozen horses moving up and down on the rods, that tinny music was playing the same tune over and over again. It sounded far away, thin and lost, like music in a dream.

They were nearing the ground, coming down and swinging backward along the bottom of the wheel, and the music was loud and harsh and they could hear the barker crying to the people, "Six rides for a dime! Six rides for a dime! See the fairgrounds! See the midway! Six rides! Step this way ... step this way ... step this way ..." And then the voice faded and was lost as they rose upward again into the dark ceiling above, upward and backward and forward and downward like a turning in the stomach. Only once it was interrupted when the wheel stopped to take on new passengers. High above the fair, their gondola swung gently.

"Gilly, Gilly ..."

She didn't look at him, but stared out through the framework of steel, the great spokes and supporting beams, down toward the lights below. "Always you're trying to say something to me, Daniel," she said quietly. "Only you never do."

He looked at her white profile against the dark, the blond hair trembling a little in the night breeze. She was troubled and distant at that moment, and he knew again that he was hurting her without wanting to. "Don't know what to say, I reckon," he said gently. "I guess I like you better than I ever liked anything."

"I'm never sure," she said. "You change so suddenly and I don't know why. I came to the fair with you and I was happy, walking along, looking at the people, hearing the music. Then something happened. I said something about Jerry and the doll looking like him—and there was a wall between us again." She hesitated a moment and added, "If it were just that you were jealous of a dead man, a man I never even loved, I could understand that. But it's something else, something more than that, something I don't know about."

"There's nothing to know."

Gilly was silent for a moment before she said, "Danny—when the sheriff was talking to me he said something about your father and how Jerry had always used it against you—"

"Wasn't just Jerry," he said grimly. "The whole town used it against me ever since I come here. Only Jerry used it most."

"Is that why you're always hitting out at people, trying to even things up?"

"How can you even up a thing like that?" Danny asked. He felt Gilly looking at him, watching him. "It wasn't Pa's fault to begin with." And then he was telling her, telling her a thing he'd never shared. "Ma was sick and the doctor wouldn't come up from Bradford. Said it was too far up the mountains, said it wasn't serious enough to get out of bed in the middle of the night. He give Pa a little bottle of pills to bring down the fever."

Danny looked down at Bradford County Fair, the lights and the pennants. "When Ma died next day, Pa took me down to Grandma's cabin. I wasn't more than ten months old, I reckon. He went into Bradford and shot the doctor, shot him dead. It took three bullets. It took them three weeks to hang him for it."

Up through the night the music came closer and went away. Danny felt sick and sad inside, sick and sad, and a little quiet too. He felt Gilly's hand touch his and Gilly's voice saying softly, "Don't be lonely, please...."

Then through the creaking steel frame of the wheel Danny saw a gondola swing downward and three people crowded together in it. They were looking back at him. He bent forward, watching their gondola swing down, down below and out of sight.

"What's wrong, Daniel?"

"How many rides we had?"

"Four or five—I lost count. They ought to be putting us off in a minute."

"Let's get off now." He turned in his seat and looked back. He could see gondola number eight swinging upward behind him, see Judd Jenkins and his wife and Martha Otis sitting in it, still watching him. They seemed to be talking. Then gondola number eight swung upward into the dark night and the bottom of the car was passing above Danny's head. When he turned, his own gondola was just passing the brakeman. He began to pull at the latch of the little door.

"Daniel, wait—you'll hurt yourself!" Gilly pulled at his arm and then the brakeman swung past and they were going upward again. "Let us off!" Danny shouted at him, but already the white face below was sinking away, away with the earth, and Danny's shout was lost. Upward, upward, faces in other gondolas turning, all the faces turning toward Danny's gondola—then Judd and Sarah and Martha again, turning in their gondola now to stare at him, still talking to each other. Danny could feel the sweat gathering on his face. "I've got to get off!"

"Daniel, stop! What's got into you?" Gilly asked, but he hardly heard her. The car was swinging over the top, far, far above the lights and the pennants and the tent tops and the tinny music. And again they were rushing down and gondola number eight was swinging up behind them. It was like being caught, caught in a nightmare where you tried to run and couldn't, where you tried to escape and couldn't. All you could do was wake up holding your hand to your throat, trying to get the air you needed to scream. "I got to wake up," Danny thought. "I got to get out of the dream. I got to get out!"

"Danny!"

"I'm being followed!" Down below, on the ground that was rising toward him, faces were turning upward. He felt the gondola swing violently under him as he arose and stepped into space. Somewhere directly above him in the darkness he heard a woman scream. Then the earth broke open and he touched it softly as a feather, touched it and awoke.

Around him and above him a vague circle of faces wavered like a reflection in water after a stone has been dropped into it. He heard a murmur at first, a murmur with a thread of tinny music running through it, then the murmur coming close with the swiftness of a comet, coming close, becoming voices: *He stood up—what happened—he fainted—no, drunk probably—the Ferris wheel, right out of the car—near thirty feet—he was acting peculiar—maybe he was sick—he jumped—why should he jump, he fell—how could he fall without standing up—maybe sick—no, drunk probably.* Then a face bent over him, a face he knew.

"Gilly," he said, "get me out of here."

"They're looking for Dr. Peabody."

"I don't want any doctor. Get me out of here."

"Are you sure?"

"Nothing's wrong with me. Get me out."

"All right, darling. I'll try."

Then he was lying back in a car seat and Gilly's face was still near him. His back felt like a slab of marble, marble that ached and throbbed. Air was streaming in across his face, and when he opened his eyes he saw a fringe of treetops swing past. It made him dizzy and he closed his eyes again.

"Whose car is this?"

"The taxi from town. It was at the gate."

Back in his mind, the circle of people floated close together and opened like a rose—just faces, none he recognized. Wearing disguises probably, he thought. Then he felt Gilly's hand in his and twisted his face away from her, toward the open window and the cold air. When he opened his eyes again he saw rooftops, the rooftops of Bradford's houses. It hurt him when he turned back toward her. In the dark Gilly's face was white and haggard, a ghost with high cheekbones and eyes dark and lost. For a long time they looked at each other.

Gilly whispered, "Why, Daniel?"

"Gilly—" He stopped and tried again. "Gilly, you were right, about me always trying to say something."

"What is it, Daniel?" Her voice was hardly a whisper. "Can you tell me now?"

"I thought I could—but I lost the words."

"Someday you'll find them."

"Someday ain't soon enough."

Then his despair closed over him again and he was back in the darkness, the impenetrable darkness, lost and feeling only the touch of a hand he could not see.

Danny's back still hurt him when he went out to Mose's a couple of nights later, but it was better walking the three miles to Blackwater plantation than lying on his bed at Aunt Jessie's thinking and waiting. He wanted to be near somebody, somebody he could talk to. And yet when he got to the plantation there didn't seem to be much to say and Mose didn't prod his thoughts out of him the way he sometimes did. Mose seemed to have things of his own to think about. After a while they both went out and sat on the step of Mose's shack, quiet, each thinking his own thoughts.

They sat like this often, the night all around them, not talking, just listening to the frogs in the swamp and watching the fireflies dancing in the dark. Sometimes Mose would sit with Mister Guitar—that was the way he called it—lying in his lap and sort of ease his fingers over the frets, touching the strings now and then with his right hand. Not music especially, not anything really, but just nighttime sounds, the kind of sounds that take a long time dying away and it seems forever that you hear them dwindling and humming into the distance, way back in the box—sounds like a man thinking, like a man cheerful, like a man remembering, like a man crying.

Behind him on the top step Mose just let his fingers trail over the gut strings like he was undecided. Then he hit a full chord, sharp and strong and definite. For a long minute the chord sort of hung there in the dark and then Mose opened his wide mouth and began to sing—quiet, to himself, like a blues song ought to be. Quiet and deep and sad.

Lonesome ...
    Lonesome ...
Steamboat whistle on the river,

Going down around the bend,
Black man waiting in the jailhouse,
Waiting for the night to end,
    Lonesome.

Lonesome ...
        Lonesome ...
I warned her not to grieve me,
Never to deceive me,
Never for to leave me,
Girl with the two white shoes,
    Lonesome.

Lonesome, lonesome. Danny looked off into the dark toward the boarded-up mansion among the trees. He wondered if Mose knew that he and Gilly sometimes came to Blackwater plantation, wondered if Mose didn't know a lot more than he sometimes told. There were some things Mose had never talked about—like what he'd done or where he'd been in the years before he came to Bradford. All the same Mose never gave anybody the feeling of a man with secrets. It was like there were some things that had happened, unhappy things maybe, but forgotten, like you bury dead people and leave them there forever. Because of that you could talk or not talk around Mose and he was still company. And when he made music—well, that was a kind of talking. Mose knew how to sing to a guitar, his throat just letting the song flow out like a river, a river in the night.

Daylight coming in the morning,
Hangman waiting on the stones,
Rope hanging from the gallows,
Pit waiting for my bones,
    Lonesome.

A deep river—sad, so sad—coming from Mose's mouth. The hands moving up the frets, the fingers catching the strings and letting the words chant over them while they died away. A guitar could sound like anything, Danny thought, but tonight it sounded like a man crying—lonesome, lonesome.

> Don't send me flowers,
> Don't send me mail,
> And where I'm going,
> I won't need bail,
>   Lonesome.

Was something bothering Mose? Was he thinking about something that had happened a long time ago, something private? Sometimes Mose got quiet. "Just comes natural," he'd say, and he'd hardly open his mouth for two or three days. Maybe this was one of those times. Since Danny had come to the plantation that night Mose hadn't said much except that one of Daisy Bell's pups had been attacked by a hen. Or was there something else bothering Mose, something not so long ago, not so private? Danny raised his head.

> Just tell my folks
> And the section crews,
> Black man's gone a-looking
> For the girl with the two white shoes,
>   Lonesome.

The song drifted off into the night and the last chord was ringing farther and farther back in the box when Danny said, "What're you singing?"

He couldn't see Mose's face in the shadow. All he heard was Mose's voice saying quietly, "A story, Daniel, a blues story."

"You're saying something."

Mose's fingers plucked at a couple of strings like he was calling back a little piece of the song. It was almost as if Danny and Mose were talking in the song, as if the song weren't over and what they were saying to each other was part of it.

"Story always say something," Mose answered.

"You're saying it to me."

"Just talk," Mose's voice said. "Talking to Mister Guitar."

"You're talking to me, but you won't speak it plain."

"What the song say?" Mose asked.

"It's about me—" Danny stopped and there was silence on the step. There was still a chance that he was wrong, a chance that the song hadn't meant anything. He asked, "How long you known?"

"Since coon hunt night," the voice said quiet in the dark, and the chance was gone.

"How you know?"

"I never saw you kick a dog before."

For a while neither one said anything. The black man's hands wandered over the strings, pulling out faraway chords, letting them drift back where they came from. He was improvising, letting the music come its own way. On the bottom step Danny stared off into the darkness, wondering why Mose had waited so long to tell him, why he wasn't afraid, why it was that instead he felt sorry for Mose, sorry that he'd hurt him. And suddenly he knew what kind of man Mose was—a black man standing up straight, not surprised by any sadness. Sadness was like a river, like the music that flowed through him, and a new sadness was like a little creek running into a big river. It didn't make much difference to the river. Maybe that was why Danny didn't feel afraid. Mose had told the truth, and because it was Mose saying it, the truth was gentle now. But what would it be like when the moon went down and the sun came up?

"You going to tell?" Danny's voice was so low-pitched he could hardly hear himself.

But he heard Mose's answer plain—"No."

"Why?"

"Figure I'll let you do the telling."

Fear, like a spasm across the stomach. "I'm not going to give myself up—if that's what you're thinking."

"You'll give yourself up, Danny."

"What makes you so sure?"

"Just know."

"Don't say you just know. Tell me reasons."

Mose bent over the guitar again, but he didn't play. "Because you ain't mean," he said. "You ain't a killer, but you killed a man, I don't know how. It ain't something you can forget or throw away. You can wash your hands clean, but you can't wash away what your eyes see inside you. You got to tell somebody, got to. Else you got to go on killing a dead man over and over and you can't do it. Because you ain't mean."

For some reason that he didn't know Danny remembered a story that he'd read once in grade school—about an Arctic explorer and how he was lost in a storm and knew that he had to keep moving to keep alive, that if he lay down to rest in the snow he was dead. That was the way it was, you had to keep moving, had to keep walking no matter how tired you were—and maybe in the end your feet would only take you to the same place anyway. It was something complicated to think about, something hard to understand, and he wanted to listen to what Mose was saying.

"Man wrote a poem once about a sailor that killed a good luck bird—an albatross—that was following his ship, and afterward the other sailors made him hang the dead bird around his neck. That was just a bird, and you killed a man, and it ain't simple. Never was. To kill you got to be God and it makes a man nervous to try to be God. Man ain't an old hound dog, but he ain't God either—he's something in between. Something between good and bad—and the thing that makes him more than a hound dog is that he knows the difference. That's why you kicked Daisy Bell, because you done something wrong and it made you afraid. You want to stop being afraid, Daniel—then go to the sheriff. Because if you don't, Jerry Sykes ain't ever going to give you no peace, no matter how long you live."

Danny was listening a long time after Mose stopped talking, trying to figure on the meaning of what Mose had said. If only he could understand, first in his head and maybe someday in his heart, maybe he'd know what to do, maybe he'd never be afraid again. Then the guitar made a mournful little sound in the night and Danny spoke, "You know what'll happen to you if they find out you knew—"

The answer, dry, soft—"I reckon."

There wasn't anything you could answer to that, anything you could say to a man who'd been your friend and would always be your friend no matter what you did. You couldn't say you knew it was him crying, not the guitar, and you couldn't say thanks. All you could do was sit there quiet, listening to the guitar, wondering how to take away the hurt in the black fingers, in the black heart.

Danny stood up. "I'm sorry I kicked your dog," he said softly.

There was no answer from the top step. Mose just bent his head over the guitar, watching his fingers move along the frets. The boy waited a moment and then walked slowly away into the darkness, down the lane between the trees. Behind him the black man's fingers moved down across the strings just once more, and lay quiet against the guitar. At last the chord vanished into the night, and Danny was alone with only the sound of his own footsteps in the dusty road.

Chapter Seven

The old clock in the courthouse cupola stood at a few minutes past eleven when Danny walked down Main Street again. He'd heard the clock chime the hour as he crossed the tracks on the road in from Blackwater. But he'd been thinking of Mose's song and what Mose had said and he hadn't heard the first strokes. All he'd heard and counted were the last four and it bothered him when he waited for the other strokes that didn't come, knowing there must be more, but hearing only the silence. At first he'd thought the clock had gone dead again and then he remembered that sometimes, in the last days particularly, he wouldn't hear people talking to him until the last words of a sentence.

That must be what dying before your time is like, he thought—just hearing a part of what you should and always waiting for the rest, always getting no answer on the silent air, always wondering what the rest would have been like. Always wondering, never knowing. If they caught him, that's the way it would be with him, the way it was with his father. You lived thirty-seven years and one day you stood on a little wooden platform that dropped away under you and then there was no more counting—no thirty-eight, no thirty-nine, no forty. If you were only twenty-three you heard less, saw less, loved less, and maybe hated less.

But about the hate Danny wasn't sure. Listening to Mose everything became sort of calm and Danny could feel himself leveling off inside. He stopped feeling afraid, stopped feeling hate, and what he felt about Gilly had a kind of soft sadness in it. And Jerry—Jerry was some distant figure in a dream, a dream in which they had fought and he had won. He couldn't remember any longer what he had felt in that moment when he lifted the rock and brought it down on Jerry's head. Not that it made a difference. Jerry was dead.

That was where Mose was wrong. Mose said you had to confess—

but what if you confessed? It wouldn't start Jerry's heart beating again. You did something wrong and maybe sometimes you admitted it, you tried to straighten it out. But what if you did something so bad you never could straighten it out? You took a man's watch, you could give it back. But if you took his life, you couldn't give him back five minutes' worth. You couldn't change your mind. If you were sorry all you could do was not do it again. What good was confessing?

Sure, Mister Law said a life for a life, an eye for an eye, a tooth for a tooth—but that was from where Mister Law sat. Mister Law didn't care about separate human beings, it was his job to care about everybody. It was his job to bring you to trial, see if you were guilty, punish you if you were, and hope it would set an example so nobody else would commit the same crime again. If Mister Law caught you he was doing his job, but if he couldn't—well, you'd gotten away with what you'd done. And getting away with a crime was different from committing it. Before you killed a man you could still stop yourself. After you'd done it, you couldn't.

Danny wished either that he could stop thinking or that he'd had more education. Took education to think about killing. Like Mose said, killing ain't simple. To kill a man you got to be God, and maybe even God felt bad about letting men die. Jehovah, they used to call him in Sunday School, and to Danny he'd always seemed like an angry God, angry and righteous. But Jehovah was supposed to know everything, more than all the college professors put together, more than Mister Law. What would Jehovah say about confessing? Would he say it paid off?

That was a tough question and you needed to be as smart as Jehovah to answer it. And right then Danny didn't feel like he was God. Maybe he had when he killed Jerry, maybe he had when he was driving the sedan, maybe when they smacked into the walls of the underpass and he knew he wasn't going to be killed by steel and concrete, maybe even when he kissed Gilly. Maybe then, but not now. Now was a time when you had to keep moving, keep answering questions. It was like the exam and you hadn't studied for it. All you saw were the questions—you never knew the answers.

Only for an exam if you failed, they gave you F on a report card. On this one they gave you a number on a picture and took your life.

Danny was so busy thinking he didn't even notice the little group of men standing around the streetlamp until he began walking along the sidewalk in front of the courthouse. He wondered why they were standing out there talking so late and then he saw the light shining down on the trash-littered wedge of lawn under the sheriff's second-floor window. Ken Williams must still be up there answering questions, sweating it out—Ken Williams, the smart guy, the guy with a new scheme for every day in the week, the guy who was going places with a fourteen-piece band. Funny how many mistakes Mister Law made. There was the guy most likely to succeed sitting in the sheriff's office and here was Danny outside, wandering around free.

Danny stopped at the edge of the little huddle of men, his face shaded from the streetlight, thinking he might hear something. Judd Jenkins was there and so were Ed Conlon and Homer Blackstone and Amos Green, the used car dealer—all standing around smoking their pipes and chewing the fat while they waited for word from the sheriff. As usual Judd Jenkins was doing most of the talking, but he wasn't talking about Ken Williams and the killing like Danny had expected. He was talking about frogs, particularly about a frog a man had brought into the hardware store a few months back.

"A regular maneater he was," Judd said. "All of twenty-one, twenty-two inches from tip to tip. First I think it's a baby crocodile. Then I see I'm mistook. Had a belly on him bigger than J. B. Sykes—could've worn a watch and chain across it. How about it, Danny?" he said, looking around. "You hunt frogs. Ever see a frog that size?"

"I gigged one seventeen inches long back in the swamp two years ago," said Danny.

"That's pretty big," said Judd. He kept on talking. "My only regret was the frog was dead—couldn't hear him sing. Man said he had a natural bass voice so deep it kind of haunted you afterward, like it was echoing in his belly."

"Suppose we could get a frog like that up to the legislature?" Homer asked. "Put it under the desk of one of them politicians. Bet when they both started talking nobody could tell the difference."

The other old men sort of chuckled to themselves over that, but nobody laughed. It was too late and cold to laugh, and besides in the backs of their minds they never forgot that the sheriff was still questioning Ken Williams. Every now and then they'd shoot a quick glance up at the sheriff's window to see if the light was still there.

"Sheriff must be onto something hot if he keeps the boy up this late," said Homer.

"Well," Judd put in, "they say if you can just tire a man out he'll always give you the truth after a while, just so he can go to sleep."

"I bet the Williams boy is sweating."

"Reckon you would too if you was in his shoes," said Ed Conlon.

Judd turned around to Danny again and said in a quiet, confidential tone of voice, but loud enough for the others to hear, "That was some little accident you had out at the fair night before last. I thought for a minute there that you was killed for sure." He lowered his voice still more. "What happened—you been drinking?"

Danny felt the eyes of all the men looking at him, felt the sudden silence that had fallen on them. "A little," he said.

Judd nodded his head as if he'd known it all the time. "That's what I told the womenfolks. A man don't get up on a Ferris wheel unless he's drunk or crazy. I figured it was most apt to be the former."

"Seems like you been having a lot of accidents lately," said Homer. "First you get in a wreck, then you fall off the Ferris wheel. You trying to kill yourself?"

"Ain't you ever had an accident without trying to kill yourself?" Danny asked.

He didn't get an answer because just then a car door slammed and a big black sedan rolled away from the side of the courthouse. "That's J. B.'s car," said Judd. "Heck and gosh-amighty! Here we been standing talking and we didn't even see him come out."

"Light's out in the sheriff's window," Homer exclaimed. He turned and looked at the others. "I wonder what the answer's going to be."

"Maybe he got the confession—you suppose?"

"Wait a minute," Ed Conlon broke in. "Somebody's coming out now."

They all looked up to the top of the courthouse steps as two men came through the swinging oak doors. "What's he bringing Williams out for?" asked Ed Conlon.

"I dunno," said Judd.

It was Ken all right, coming down the steps with the sheriff. He was wearing a red button sweater and flannel pants that were wrinkled and baggy like he'd been wearing them steady for a long time or even slept in them. He must have caught sight of the men under the streetlamp because when he and the sheriff got to the bottom of the steps he walked away in the opposite direction. Then Clem walked up to the group, pulling his light coat around him. "Waiting up, boys?" he asked. "What you want to know?"

"I just see Ken Williams walk off down the street like he was free as the rest of us," Homer said. "How come?"

"Because he's got the same rights to be on the streets as anybody else. I been questioning him fourteen hours steady today and fourteen hours yesterday. I got no evidence against him so I let him go—that's all."

"You let him go and you ain't even got another suspect to take his place?" asked Judd. "Don't sound sensible to me."

"Can't hold a man just because you need a culprit," said Clem.

"All the same," Judd came back, "what's the town going to think when they find out you been questioning the wrong man for two days and ain't got nothing to show for it. And the real killer still walking the streets of Bradford maybe."

"Maybe," said the sheriff. "Could be anybody—maybe you, maybe me. Anyway, till I catch the man that did it, I don't know any more than you fellers."

"If you don't know any more than we do," asked Homer, "what the heck are we paying you for, Sheriff?"

The sheriff looked over at Homer and smiled kind of gentle. "For what Bradford pays the sheriff," he said quietly, "I oughtn't to use more than one-tenth of my brains."

The men didn't say any more right away but they didn't like it a bit. They'd thought there was going to be a quick, easy answer to the killing and now they found out it wasn't going to be so simple. In their heads they'd already put Ken on the stand, brought witness against him, and convicted him. Now they were going to have to rearrange the facts. Besides they didn't like the sheriff to tell them they were wrong. They began to move off, kind of muttering to themselves, and Danny tagged along with them, thinking: That's the way they'd be talking about me if I'd been up in the sheriff's office instead of Ken.

Judd was walking along near him, shaking his head and arguing with himself, when suddenly he raised his head. "I near forgot," he said to Danny. "That knife you lost. Billy Scripture had it this evening. He was standing with us in front of the courthouse just before you came along. Trying to whittle with it, he was."

Danny just kept looking ahead. "How could it have been my knife?" he asked.

"Must have found it somewheres—maybe one of those times he went hunting with you."

"Maybe Billy found a knife. That don't mean it's my knife," said Danny.

"Couldn't be anybody else's," said Judd firmly. "Never had but two of that type of knife in the first place. One I sold to you last spring. The other's still setting up in the store."

"Maybe." Danny didn't make any more of it because the sheriff was walking behind them. He pretended he was taking a short cut home and separated himself from the others. He crossed the street and waited under the trees until Clem and Ed and Judd and Homer had gone out of sight. Then he began walking back past the courthouse, out along Main Street toward the secondhand furniture store where Billy Scripture lived. He hurried as fast as he could, not passing anybody, but when he neared the dirt road that crossed Main Street he slowed down. Up ahead, Billy Scripture was limping under the last streetlight on his way home.

Limping home under the streetlamp Billy felt, as he always did, the bitterness and resentment of a child being put to bed. The beautiful day was gone and he was alone now in the night when nothing ever happened. Each day was full of surprises and wonder, of bright things lying in the trash heaps along the alleys, of houses being built, of locomotives coming into the station, of children playing, of people walking on Main Street. But the night was different. Night was a time of tiredness, of carpenters locking their tool chests and shopkeepers closing their doors, of people leaving Main Street, of children called in to supper. It was a time of the sun going down, a time of cold, a time of being alone.

Night meant an end of surprises, an end of everything until morning. Night was a defeat he could not understand. It came down like the sudden and vexatious lowering of a curtain. Somehow Billy always tried to keep the curtain up, to make the play go on, but he always failed. In the late afternoon he usually sat among the other men in the gloomy back corner of Jenkins' Hardware, watching their lips move and sometimes grinning when they grinned. But always there came a time when one of the men would get up and stretch, and that was the moment when Billy would dig into his pocket and bring out a broken bit of glass or a radiator cap and thrust it out, hoping to entice someone to remain. Sometimes one of the men would fondle the bit of trash for a moment, then hand it back with a smile. Usually they just grinned and shook their heads and went out the door in ones and twos, leaving Billy alone among the mops and galvanized tin pails, waiting for the moment when Judd would tap him on the shoulder.

When that happened Billy would get up and limp very slowly across the wooden floor to the door. He never turned, never made a gesture of goodbye. He didn't like being put out like a dog or a cat, and way back in his three-year-old mind he resented Judd for closing his store and pulling down the big window curtains.

He would go down Main Street then to George's Eat Café and sit at a counter stool near the little window where the cook passed the food through from the kitchen. Billy never ordered. George simply brought him the soup and later the meat and mashed potatoes and peas. For dessert Billy always ate apple pie à la mode, because once George had put a dip of vanilla on the pie as a special favor and Billy would never eat pie without ice cream again. While he ate Billy would set the bit of glass or radiator cap next to his plate, and sometimes he would touch it gravely with his fingers. Then George would punch his meal ticket and Billy would pick up his toy and go out to the street again.

After that he might go across the street to the motion picture theater and watch the enormous figures from the front row until the light from the screen hurt his eyes, or he might catch a ride to some roadhouse with a jukebox, or if he was very lucky, Danny might take him along on a coon hunt. But always, sooner or later, he had to go home, down toward the railroad tracks to the little lean-to built on the back of Joe Weeper's secondhand furniture store. Usually he was cold and tired then, hardly seeing things anymore, hardly interested even in the toy he carried in his pocket. And the lights in the houses along the street made him feel even lonelier than ever.

But on his way home there was always one thing that filled him with a soft and inexpressible amazement. He never searched for it and yet he always knew when he was coming near, and close to the last streetlight where the sidewalk suddenly ended and became a dirt path he would look down, and there in the concrete was a footprint much smaller than his own. Billy no longer remembered the child or the day that the child had carefully pressed its foot in the wet concrete, and yet each night when he came to the footprint in the walk he tried his own foot in it. It was a long time now since his own foot had fitted the impression, and all he could do now was stand on it. But even just standing there he was filled with a curious assurance and pride, something private, a secret that was always there. But it was a secret whose meaning he had forgotten just as he had forgotten that the print was the print of his own foot.

Billy's mind was full of secrets like that, secrets without meaning— like the piece of satin under his pillow which always reminded him of being held in the arms of a woman wearing a smooth shiny dress, but warm and soft underneath, a thing that always made him a little sleepy, a little hungry, when he remembered. Like the knife with the shaggy handle that reminded him of the doll, the wonderful doll that the girl had given him at the fair. Billy never touched the knife without thinking of the doll or looked at the doll without thinking of the knife. Why, he didn't know. Only sometimes, without quite knowing what it was, the doll seemed to remind him of something else, of *somebody*, somebody whose arm had dropped back loose as a doll's when Billy had raised it to pick up the knife.

It was the knife now that made him remember the doll and made him pull his half-useless leg after him in faster, awkward steps. He lingered only a moment at the impression in the sidewalk, placing his own foot over it out of habit, then hurried on into the dark path leading toward the railroad tracks and the secondhand furniture store owned by Joe Weeper. Joe had been Billy's guardian for the past seventeen years. He was a kind man, but a careless one, and ever since his wife's death eight years before, Joe had spent most of his time drinking. By eleven o'clock of an evening he would be lying in his bed, the great Victorian gilt bed which no one would buy from him, drunk as a lord. He was asleep now as Billy went toward the rear of the store, into the yard with its old mattresses and broken bits of furniture, to the door that hung loose on its hinges. Billy lifted the latch—the door was never locked—and walked in.

The air was close in there, and dark. There was a smell of old ashes, ashes that spilled from the grate of the potbellied stove, mingled with the harsh sour smell of old varnished wood, the thousand and one bits of junk, of rusted iron and crumpled rag, that Billy had collected and never thrown away. Billy could not see but rather felt his way among the heaps of trash to the bed, and there he fumbled among the crumpled quilts until he found the doll—safe, where he had left it. At last he went back to the table in the center of the room and carefully lit the kerosene lamp. As the moisture evaporated in the glass chimney and the yellow light fell on the trash-filled room, Billy raised his eyes and felt his heart leap in him.

Across the lamp stood Danny.

Billy just stared, not quite sure if the visitor in the room was Danny or merely a ghost that he had imagined. He had played with imaginary things so long that Billy was no longer always sure where the unreal world ended and the real one began. Carefully he moved one hand outward, felt it touch the cloth of Danny's jacket—and he smiled. No smile answered him, but that did not matter. Billy was grateful to be with people even when they scolded him or rebuked him as if he were a child. He liked attention—and now Danny had come to visit him alone. For the first time someone had come into his room to share his secrets, to share his treasures.

Then Danny did a puzzling thing. He moved toward Billy and quickly ran his hands through his pockets as if he were looking for something. He lifted the lamp from the table and began to search the drawer in the table, the old broken chair, the heaps of trash. Billy followed him, pulling out a broken headlamp, a bent bicycle wheel, a shard of earthenware, a sewing machine spool. He offered them all to Danny, but Danny pushed them aside.

At last Danny spoke without any sound that reached Billy's deaf brain. Billy watched the other's mouth as he had often watched the loungers in the back of Jenkins' Hardware, wondering what it was that made them laugh, what made their faces frown or turn sad or surprised. He had seen men's lips move and other men turn and answer. What had happened to make the second man turn around? Billy didn't know. In his world there were no sounds and there never had been, although sometimes when he was very excited he felt a tightening, an agitation in his throat. All Billy knew was that in his soundless world people moved in curious and unexplainable ways and often only because by lip movement they had communicated something to each other.

Billy wished that he could understand what Danny was trying to tell him now. It was important because if he didn't understand Danny might go away, and he wanted Danny to stay. Suddenly he limped to the bed and drew back the covers. The doll, the beautiful doll, lay there quite still. Gently he picked it up, cradling it in his arms before he held it out like an offering to Danny. For a long, anxious moment Billy thought that Danny was going to refuse the doll. Then Danny slowly reached out his hand, took the doll and turned it from side to side, looking at it. But Danny raised his eyes to Billy and began to untie the scarf from the doll. He took off the cap and unbuttoned the coat. Billy smiled and nodded his head in delight. It was a game. A new game.

As he watched it seemed to Billy that he had played this game before. There was something here half recognized, a pleasure such as he felt when he placed his foot on the sidewalk imprint he had made so many years ago, a pleasure familiar yet lost and far away and part forgotten. Now Danny was placing the doll back on the bed, its arms behind its back. He crumpled the quilt about it, then moved back from the bed and looked at Billy. Billy turned his eyes back to the doll, trying to remember the game. There was something about the doll that made him think he had seen it before, long ago in some distant time that his mind couldn't remember.

He looked again at Danny who was watching him. Was it a game? Billy was confused. And when something confused him, Billy always turned to something simpler. But what? Danny was going to leave, he thought—Danny would go away and never come back unless he could find a way of keeping him, of enticing him with some bright toy.

He remembered the knife.

He put his hand inside his shirt, felt the shaggy handle in his hand. He half drew it out, then stopped. Was this the game? He wasn't sure, he couldn't remember. He looked at the doll again and it seemed that there was something familiar about it, its eyes wide open with painted lashes. Then without quite knowing why, Billy took out the knife and carefully, tentatively, laid it at the foot of the doll. Was it right? But as he looked at Danny for confirmation, a tremor passed through him. Danny was moving toward him, moving toward the knife.

At that moment Billy knew that Danny wanted the knife, that he meant to take it. He limped in front of Danny, recovered the knife. What happened next, Billy didn't understand. For suddenly he felt the full weight of Danny's body thrown against him and Danny's hands were at his throat, shaking him. He closed his eyes in dizziness. When he opened them, Danny's face was close to his, he could feel Danny's breath, and Danny's eyes were angry, like the terrible animals Billy sometimes dreamed were trampling him.

Billy stumbled back under Danny's rush and fell clumsily against the wall beside the stove. Danny's hands were tighter now on his throat and Billy couldn't breathe at all. A sudden great fear passed through him. Looking at Danny's eyes and face, he knew that Danny's hands were never going to let go, that he would never breathe again. He tried weakly to raise his body but there was no strength in it, only the weakness of his own fear. Again Danny shook him until Billy's head half rested against the wall. Suddenly the light from the lamp fell full upon Billy's face, blinding him.

It was then that a curious thing happened—like everything else, Billy didn't know why—but all of a sudden Danny stopped shaking him. Somewhere in the shadow was Danny's face and it was hidden from Billy. All he knew was that for just a moment Danny's hands had loosened slightly on his throat and now they were taken away and a great painful rush of air poured into Billy's breaking lungs. As he stayed against the wall, gasping for breath, Billy's chest heaved up and down painfully. He felt the hands touch him again, the hands that a moment ago had been choking him, and he cringed. But the hands were different now, straightening his clothes, helping him to his feet. Danny had been angry because he had done something wrong, something he didn't know. But now Danny wasn't angry anymore and his hands were gentler and kinder than any hands that had ever touched him.

Still standing at the wall, Billy saw Danny go back to the bed, pick up the fallen knife from the cover, and walk to the door. There he turned again. Billy stared at him with wide-open eyes, not knowing whether Danny would come back and strike him or not. Then Danny's hand lifted in a sudden motion and tossed the knife back onto the bed. For a moment longer they watched each other, then Billy smiled and Danny turned quickly. The door closed and Billy was alone.

Billy stayed half crouched against the wall for a long time afterward, not moving. He felt afraid and hurt and puzzled. He had played the game wrong and Danny had punished him. But what had he done wrong? That he would never know. In this inexplicable world where people put you out of a door at sundown and answered communications that he did not understand, Billy had long ago learned simply to accept things as they were, no matter how strange. All he knew was that Danny was gone and he was alone with only the doll and that there would be no more surprises till morning.

The sheriff was tired after the fourteen hours he'd spent questioning Ken Williams. He'd felt from the beginning that he was barking up the wrong tree and yet he'd had to cover all the angles so there wouldn't be any doubts in his own mind. Watching Ken sweat over the normal mistakes that come under close questioning, he'd felt sorry for the boy and he was glad to let him go. And walking alone now under the dark elms toward his house, Clem suddenly realized something that left him half ashamed. Deep in his heart he knew that he didn't want to find the man who'd killed Jerry Sykes, that never in all his years as sheriff had he really wanted to catch a man for a crime. He suddenly wished that he had become anything in the world, a farmer or a veterinary or a storekeeper like Judd Jenkins, anything but a human bloodhound. That was what rankled him when the townspeople got on his heels for not doing better on a job he hated. And yet Clem knew he'd done a good job and so did the town.

Funny about people, Clem thought to himself—they were too eager to punish. People didn't really care about catching criminals to protect society. What they cared about was the punishment, reading the details of a trial or an execution, talking them over and over. There was something cruel in people that made them like to see somebody hurt, and if it was a criminal, then it was justified. Just like a war gave you a right to kill as many men as you could, a crime committed gave you the right to kill the criminal and everybody could enjoy reading about it in the papers and feel very righteous. Somehow Clem had never been able to feel righteous—maybe because he'd seen too much human nature, seen too many thieves or killers who'd been sick inside, sick human beings. The dividing line between the righteous and unrighteous, the well and the sick, the quick and the dead, was pretty thin sometimes.

But thin or not, Clem had his duty and he had to do his best. Once more he turned his mind heavily to the Jerry Sykes killing. There still wasn't much to go on, past the main fact that the boy was dead. Clem would have to go back for motives. Not money— Ken had explained all that. What about vengeance? There were a lot of people around Bradford with reasons to dislike Jerry, but hardly reasons strong enough to kill him. Jealousy?

Clem was certain that Gilly had had nothing to do with the killing and yet it kept coming back into his mind that the schoolteacher might be somewhere at the center of it. When two people were in love with the same person you had a motive, but Gilly hadn't seemed to be connected with anybody in a way as important as love. From the way Clem figured it, Jerry had never really amounted to a hill of beans as far as Gilly was concerned. As for young Daniel, Gilly had explained how she came to go home with him the night Jerry disappeared. Nothing remarkable about a girl catching a ride home—but it was curious they should bob up again on a Ferris wheel. Did Danny really fall from the wheel or had he jumped? And if he'd jumped, why? Might be an answer there.

He was a strange one, Daniel was, always had been. But he'd never done anything you could blame him for and you couldn't hang a man for being less sociable than other folks. He'd been deviled plenty about his father by a lot of folks and particularly by Jerry, but he'd always taken it kind of quiet by drawing back into himself. One of the reasons Clem had kept his mind off Danny was just because he was such an easy suspect—the son of a criminal, or what folks called a criminal. And yet?

The sheriff shook his head. Trouble was you could explain everything separately but when you put it all together it made a picture, a picture with part of it torn away and missing. Like the knife. Danny had lost a knife and had tried to replace it, and yet when Judd had told him Billy Scripture had it, Danny didn't want to admit it was his. Where had Billy found the knife? He was on the coon hunt the night they found the body. Had he found the knife there? If he had, nobody would ever know. Billy wasn't the kind of witness you could put on the stand and get the same evidence twice—if any.

The sheriff turned in at his own gate and went toward the steps. He was tired of thinking, tired of his job, tired of Judd and Homer and the others needling him. If only Martha would keep her mouth shut and leave him alone.

But Martha was in no mood to keep her mouth shut. The minute Clem came in the door she turned off the radio. "Well?" she asked.

Clem didn't answer her question. "Any milk in the house?" he said. "I'd like a bowl of milk and crackers before I go to bed."

"Plenty of milk in the icebox," Martha answered. "There's crackers on the second shelf."

The sheriff walked into the kitchen and took the milk from the icebox. He poured it into a soup bowl, carefully crumbled five crackers into it. He thought for a moment of staying in the kitchen and eating it in peace, but he knew Martha wouldn't let him have it. He went back into the parlor to the big leather chair and set the bowl on the table beside it.

Martha waited until he'd put the first spoonful in his mouth and then she said irritably, "I asked you a question five minutes ago, Clem Otis, and you haven't yet seen fit to answer it. Did the Williams boy confess yet?"

"No," said Clem. "The Williams boy didn't confess."

Martha seemed annoyed about that. "Well, I can't understand how he has the gumption to sit there and keep saying he didn't do it when the facts are plain as day."

"Why should a man confess," Clem asked tiredly, putting his spoon back into the mush and stirring it a little, "if he's innocent?"

"Now Clem"—Martha's voice had a tone of false patience—"you don't mean to say that boy's innocent when the whole town thinks different!"

Why did women's voices become so unpleasant after forty, Clem wondered, but didn't say it out loud. Instead he said, "The town doesn't know the facts and neither do you, Martha. I've questioned the boy for nearly thirty hours altogether and he's innocent as you or me."

"Don't mention me in the same breath as that murderer," Martha said indignantly. She leaned forward in her chair again. "I'll bet if you let me in there with that boy I'd have you a confession in short order."

"It's a little late, Martha," said the sheriff. "I've already let him go."

"Clem Otis, you haven't!"

"And now, Martha," said the sheriff, getting up with the empty bowl, "if you'll keep your mouth shut for five consecutive minutes I'm going to bed."

"Clem, you're not going to bed until you've locked every door and window in this house!"

"What for?"

"Why, with that Williams boy walking around the streets I wouldn't sleep a wink tonight for fear of being murdered in my bed."

"You're a foolish woman, Martha."

"I'd like to know who's more foolish—you or me," Martha kept chattering. "One of the finest boys in town has been murdered and you go around releasing the man who did it."

"Sure is remarkable," said Clem dryly, "how dying can make a saint of a man."

"Well, maybe Jerry did have his faults," said Martha. "But he was settling down all the same. Going right steady with that schoolteacher he was. Nobody would have been a bit surprised if he up and married her."

"I suppose that's what all you old hens jabber about at the Ladies' Aid every week?"

"Who're you calling an old hen?"

"Come to bed, Martha—come to bed."

They went upstairs. The sheriff sat on the edge of the bed while Martha put on her curlers in the bathroom. She kept on talking, but Clem had stopped listening, stopped thinking even. His back hurt and he was almost too tired to take off his shoes and lower his suspenders. By the time he'd gotten into his nightshirt and climbed into bed, Martha had come out of the bathroom. Clem took one look at her and turned away. When she's young a woman shows her best side to her husband, but when she's older she shows her best side to strangers, the sheriff thought.

"How can you sleep with all those contraptions on your head?" he asked.

"I've got to do something to keep up my appearance," said Martha. On the other side of the bed Clem could feel Martha pull up the covers and let in a draft as she got into bed. "Old hen," she repeated spitefully. "Well, a woman makes her bed, she has to lie in it, I suppose. But I'll say this, Clem Otis—I sure underestimated your possibilities when I went to the altar with you."

"Go to sleep, for heaven's sake," said the sheriff.

But Martha had to have the last word. "As for Jerry—I think he was a lot better than the girl he was going after. She sure didn't wait long to tie up with another boy. Shows how sincere she was."

Martha turned over on her side, her back to Clem, and settled down after that. The sheriff lay back on his pillow, grateful for the silence—only he wished that the throbbing would stop behind his eyeballs. Then suddenly he opened his eyes again.

"Martha," he said. "Martha!"

"What is it?"

"Who is Gilly Johnson tied up with?"

"Heaven sakes, Clem—with Jessie Hawkins' nephew."

"Been keeping steady company?"

"Lydia Simpkins says they been thick as fleas ever since Jerry disappeared."

"When d'you hear this?"

"Lydia told us at the Ladies' Aid meeting. Must have kept it mighty secret because it was the first I heard of it. Hardly believed it till I saw them together at the fair."

The sheriff was silent as Martha turned her face back on the pillow. "What makes you so interested in old hens' gossip all of a sudden?" she asked.

"Nothing, Martha, nothing. Go to sleep."

The sheriff lay back again on his pillow and after a while Martha's snoring became loud and regular. But the sheriff didn't sleep for a long time. He lay awake thinking. I know who the killer is, he said to himself. It's as plain as the nose on my face. But how am I going to prove it? How am I going to make him tell?

I nearly killed him, Danny thought to himself. I nearly killed him and he didn't know why. Lying under his quilt, Danny felt the sweat pour off him, heard his heart thumping against his chest slow and hard. His arms were rigid at his sides almost as if they were paralyzed. He moved his fingers stiffly to prove that they were still there, still capable of feeling. A sudden tremor of sickness passed through him, shaking his body. I nearly killed Billy, he thought, I nearly killed Billy and he didn't know what it was all about.

Downstairs the grandfather clock struck three times in the dark house. Then all was quiet and Danny again heard the hard, anguished beating of his heart. Sooner or later, he knew, he was going to have to start moving, go some place far from Bradford. But right now he couldn't think about it. All he could think about was Billy's face when the lamp struck it and showed his eyes—a baby's eyes trying to understand why somebody was hurting him, trying to understand and not quite making it. Sometime—he didn't know whether it was then or later—Mose's line had crossed his mind: "You ain't mean. You can't do it. You can't go on killing a dead man over and over in your mind."

Maybe. Maybe you could go on killing a dead man over and over in your mind. He wasn't sure. But what happened when you found yourself killing a helpless guy who'd always followed you around like a pet dog, a guy who didn't know anything? Ever since he'd come to Bradford he'd kept an eye on Billy, tried to protect him against the wise guys who thought it was funny not to have a full-grown brain, not to be able to talk or hear. They'd play tricks on Billy and laugh, and sometimes Billy, who was too dumb to know that the joke was on him, would smile too. Danny had hit guys for that. But what they'd done was nothing—nothing at all. He'd tried to kill Billy, a guy that didn't even have sense enough to lift his fists. Maybe if Billy had lifted his fists Danny would have killed him. And that was what made Danny lie in bed and sweat as the tremors shook his body.

I'm sick, he thought. Either I'm sick or I'm not tough enough. Maybe this is the thing I never figured. You do something, you tell a lie, and then you got to tell a lot of lies to cover the first one. You kill a man and then you got to protect the first killing. It piles up. Pretty soon you're carrying a mountain.

Well, he was going to take a powder. He hadn't known it when he'd thrown the knife back on the bed. He hadn't known it when he didn't kill Billy. But he knew it afterward. He'd gone to Billy to get the knife, to find out if that baby brain of his could remember where he'd found it, if that baby brain had ever put two and two together, if Billy could ever make a gesture that would tell the sheriff anything. Well, he'd found out. Billy could—if you put it to him right. It was a long chance, but it was there and sooner or later somebody, either the sheriff or somebody else, would put that two and two together and add it up and spell the answer. The minute Billy put the knife beside the doll, Danny had a choice. Either he took the knife and killed Billy or he left town. Not much of a choice. You were guilty either way.

That was the thing about it. He'd already killed a man and maybe they would hang him for it. They couldn't hang him twice for killing the second man. Why hadn't he killed Billy? That was the question, and when he answered it Danny didn't feel better, he felt worse. I like the kid, he thought to himself, I like him. I don't want to hurt him and I hurt him. Mose was right—I ain't tough enough. And he remembered how tired his hands had felt when he looked at Billy's face in the lamplight, too tired to do anything. He was tired of trying to cover himself, tired of behaving like he was just like anybody else in the town when in his heart he knew something awful.

He got up and put on his clothes. He put on the heaviest clothes he had because, he thought, I might have to sleep in them for a while, and it'll be cold nights.

Then he went down the stairs quietly, with his shoes in his hand, and out the back door into the yard. Around him the town was silent and cold in the hours before dawn as he stood in the darkness under the mulberry tree. I come to Bradford thirteen years ago, he thought, and now I'm leaving it and I won't eat no more mulberries off this tree. Maybe some other tree, some other place—but where? He'd have to answer that soon.

He still didn't know the answer as he went through the back gate, latched it carefully, and moved down the alley on the dark side. Somewhere a dog barked as he went, but he hardly paused. You ain't so smart, dog, he told himself. You're barking, but you don't know who you're barking at.

Chapter Eight

There weren't any more folks than usual loitering around the front of the courthouse next morning, but watching them from the window of his second-floor office Sheriff Otis thought: That's the way it always begins. First the scattered handful of curious loafers, then the little groups that grow larger as the talk grows louder, then merge, becoming a crowd. He had felt that pressure before, like a silent hand pushing you gently and with ever-increasing firmness toward action, toward taking steps you weren't ready to take. And if you didn't take them, anything could happen—and sometimes had. He'd seen a man, a word, change a restless but law-abiding crowd into a mob, something as terrible and swift as fire. It was too late to talk of patience then.

But there were other pressures. Behind him the coroner was talking. "I think you've gone plumb crazy on this case," Jake was saying. "You had a likely suspect and you let him go in favor of a brainless idiot who can't count his fingers, and you accuse him of murder!"

Without turning from the window Clem could see the coroner's potato-colored face scowling at the end of a cigar, his unlaundered striped shirt, his dirty celluloid collar. Why was it coroners didn't wash more often? Disappointed surgeons probably, Clem thought. No spark left in them, not even enough to keep their pants pressed.

"I'm not accusing Billy Scripture of anything," Clem said. "I'm just holding him."

"What's the difference?"

"I don't think you'd understand even if I told you."

"Probably not," Jake grunted sourly. He thought for a minute. "All right," he said. "Suppose you were right in letting Williams go—suppose you were a hundred per cent right. You still had enough simple facts to make a showing in front of a jury."

You're arguing like a man protecting his profession, Clem thought, but didn't say it. Instead he asked, "What's a simple fact, Jake?" He turned and stared at the untidy room before he went to the desk and ruffled his hands through the scattered papers looking for a cigar. He didn't find it and wandered back to the window.

"A man's dead—that's a fact," said Jake. "The simplest fact there is."

"What was the cause of death?"

"Depressed fracture of the skull, subdural hemorrhage," Jake answered. "It's on the report."

"Then he didn't drown or drop dead of a heart attack or die in bed with pneumonia."

"He was struck with a rock," said Jake. "What's that got to do with the subject?"

"All I'm saying, Jake," said the sheriff, "is that there isn't any such thing as a simple fact. A fact can be the most complicated thing there is, it's got as many angles as a fly has eyes. Jerry Sykes is dead, but he didn't die of natural causes. If he had they would have nailed him in a box, held a nice funeral and sent him off to the cemetery, said a prayer for him, and left him among the other peaceful folks. But he was a different kind of dead man. He was murdered. Would you say murder was a simple fact?"

Jake squinted up through the smoke that drifted from the cigar firmly clamped between his teeth. "I won't answer that. But I can tell you what the law says—"

"I know what the law says," Clem interrupted with a tired wave of his hand. "Premeditation, first degree; with qualifying cause or momentary aberration, second degree. It don't go deep enough, nowhere deep enough."

"Sounds like you want to rewrite the law."

"No," said Clem, hardly taking notice of the coroner's crack. "I ain't smart enough for that. But I'm smart enough to know that the law is wrong when it pins all the responsibility for a crime on the man who's committed one."

"How else you going to operate?"

Clem didn't hear the question; he was too busy looking for an answer to his own thoughts. After a while he said slowly, "I knew a man once kept accusing his wife of being unfaithful. After listening to him for twelve years she was."

Jake laughed harshly, showing his stained teeth. "Proved he was right. He was just a little premature—that's all."

Clem looked at the other seriously. "I say the husband not only contributed, but was directly responsible for what his wife did."

"You expect the law to go into hair-splitting like that when it's hardly got time to look at the facts?" asked Jake. "When there ain't a court in the country that hasn't got more cases on the docket than it can handle?"

"Well, somebody's got to," Clem said. He ruffled the papers on his desk again futilely, at last took the cigar Jake offered him. "Murder is like love, Jake. It takes two to commit it—the killer and the killed, the man who hates and the man who's hated. Sometimes I think that if you were to go into all the reasons why that rock struck Jerry Sykes's head you might wind up writing the history of the world."

"It's easier to stick to facts," said Jake, "and a lot more practical."

"More practical?" Clem asked. "I doubt it. Every day we're creating the men that tomorrow we're going to try for murder, crime, making wars even. And tomorrow we'll sit behind a bench and look down at them with righteousness all over our faces and say they're guilty. If we were honest we'd take part of the guilt on our own shoulders, place ourselves on trial at the same time. Maybe we'd find out a little more about why men commit crime."

"What, for instance?"

"Prejudice, for instance. Sick ways of thinking. We don't have any slums in Bradford to make criminals, but there's enough hate and prejudice in this town to account for more murders than Jerry Sykes's."

Jake looked up at Clem with a smile twisting a corner of his mouth. "You should have been a preacher, Clem, not a bloodhound."

"No," said Clem, "not a preacher. A scientist maybe. If I was younger that's what I would have gone into, I think—studying human beings, a psychologist maybe. All I know now is that a human being never was a simple fact, that a human being and what made him is a lot more than what you cut out of him on the autopsy table, Jake."

"Not when they're dead."

Clem smiled grimly as he stood near the window again, watching the loiterers. Jake was a bitter man; he didn't like to think about other human beings' problems because he'd gotten tired and bitter thinking about his own. He knew he was finished, that he'd never be anything more than a back country coroner, and the knowledge had made a selfish, cruel, and careless man out of him.

But maybe it would be Jake who would turn out to be right and Clem who'd turn out to be the fool. What did he know about human beings after all? Maybe it would be a lot simpler to bring the Hawkins boy up and sweat it out of him, like he had with Ken Williams. Maybe he was a fool to think he could trip Daniel Hawkins' conscience by pretending he wanted evidence against the deaf-mute. Maybe he didn't have a right to use Billy Scripture as a decoy, to bring him to the courthouse and let the town think what it would, hoping all the time that Daniel would stand up and confess to save the idiot from a charge the sheriff never really intended to make. Hoping—

On the desk the telephone rang twice before the sheriff heard it. He went over, picked up the receiver.

It was George, the deputy he'd sent to bring in Daniel. Clem listened close for a minute, staring at the bottom of Jake's shoes propped on the edge of his desk. He didn't dare look at Jake's face just then. Finally Clem said quietly into the phone, "Check the railroad station, then bring the schoolteacher over right away."

For a moment after he'd put down the receiver Clem vacantly read over a sheriff's order for repossession of a sewing machine for nonpayment of installments. Then he got up.

Jake twisted in his chair. "Where you going?"

"To let the deaf-mute out," said Clem matter-of-factly. "Want to come along?"

"Damn it, will you tell me why all this happened in the first place?" asked Jake, getting up reluctantly. "Some cock-and-bull theory of yours probably."

"I had an idea," Clem said. "It was wrong. Sometimes human nature don't jump in the direction we expect it to. Come on."

The sheriff opened the door and went into the hall without getting an answer from Jake. But it seemed to him that as he had passed the coroner on his way out there had been just the trace of a smile on Jake's tired, cynical face.

He knew she was there before he wheeled around in his swivel chair and looked at her—a straight, average height girl in a mannish topcoat, blond hair and gray eyes, a face that was both beautiful and plain. What you saw was the plainness first, and if you passed her on the street you might not turn around to look again, but if you did you would look for a long time.

"Sit down please, Miss Johnson," Clem said quietly, nodding to the chair the coroner had used. He watched her as she sat down without answering, holding herself very erect in the chair. "You uneasy about something?" he asked.

"I've never been in a sheriff's office before." Her voice had the huskiness that comes with tension.

Clem smiled a little. "Not much different from any other office, is it? Except it's more untidy maybe."

"That isn't it."

"Forget I'm wearing a badge," Clem said gently. "It'll make things easier."

"Why did you call me here?" Gilly asked, as if she had hardly heard Clem's attempt to make her feel easy.

Clem looked at her. The girl's eyes answered his, unwavering. "I got a problem, Miss Johnson. I thought maybe you could help me."

"If I can."

"I think you can."

She waited. Clem leaned back in the swivel chair, noticed that it was squeaking again. "How long have you known Daniel Hawkins?"

He pretended not to notice the sudden involuntary widening of her eyes, nor the sharply troubled look that darkened them. Nor did he seem to notice the uncertainty that slowed her answer. Clem was quite sure she would tell the truth because as the questioner he held an advantage. She did not know how much knowledge he already possessed, how quickly he could reveal a lie.

"Not very long," she said at last, her voice suddenly pitched so low it was almost inaudible.

"Since that night he brought you home from the dance, wasn't it?"

"That's right."

"Folks say you've been seeing the boy right regular ever since."

Again she hesitated before answering. "Pretty often."

"Usually a couple starts going together," Clem said dryly, "it doesn't take the town—the Ladies' Aid, anyway—twenty-four hours to catch on."

"That's the trouble."

"Why'd you try to keep it a secret?"

Gilly kept her gaze fixed on her hand as it straightened a fold in her coat. "Well, after the wreck and with me teaching in the school, it just seemed simpler, I guess."

"It never come into your mind that there might be some other reason for keeping it secret?"

Gilly lifted her head. "What kind of reason?"

Again Clem smiled gently. "I asked you the question."

"I don't know."

"You aren't helping me much, Miss Johnson."

The gray eyes were looking at him now, steadily. Good gray eyes, truthful eyes, but troubled—as if they were afraid of being hurt. "I don't know what you want me to say."

"Nothing but the truth," Clem said. He swung slowly around in his chair till he was looking away from her, toward the window and the sunshine outside. He wanted to make the answer to the next question easy for her. "You in love with Daniel Hawkins?"

The answer followed at once. "Yes."

"What would you say if I told you Daniel killed Jerry Sykes?"

He turned his chair till he faced her again, found the gray eyes still steady. "I wouldn't believe it." Her voice was not much more than a whisper, a defiant whisper. And yet there was something lacking, the sheriff thought—surprise.

"Because you wouldn't want to believe it," he said.

"No," she said, and suddenly her voice was full and free. "Because he's not hard like he pretends, because inside he's gentle and lonely and lost, because the town never made a place for him—never let him forget his father died like a criminal, because all his life he's had to feel ashamed for what he was—"

The sheriff got up from his chair, walked around the desk, and stood near her. "I know all that," he said quietly. "That's the reason I want Daniel to come back and confess of his own will."

The eyes looked up at him sharply. "Come back?"

"Daniel Hawkins ran away from Bradford sometime last night." He saw her eyes waver as he watched her closely. "He didn't say anything to you about going away?"

She shook her head. "No."

"No idea where he might have gone?"

"No."

"When you used to see him you must have gone someplace. Where?"

She looked away from him before she answered. "No place—only the roads at night."

"No special place?"

Again, the slow answer. "No special place." Suddenly she turned on him, the gray eyes burning with deep anger. "What are you trying to get from me, Sheriff? What are you trying to make me say? You want me to help you, you say. But why? So you can hound him like he's been hounded all his life?"

"It isn't me I want you to help, Miss Johnson," said Clem softly. "It's Daniel Hawkins that needs it."

"What makes you so sure he did it?" The voice was still defiant, but less certain.

"His own action, the way he's behaved ever since the dance. And now his running away. A man with a clear conscience doesn't very often run away."

"Maybe he didn't run away. Maybe he just went someplace—" She hesitated. "Hunting, maybe."

Clem sighed. "We're wasting time, Miss Johnson," he said wearily.

He stared for a moment at the sunshine slanting through the window behind his chair. He turned to her once more. "You say you love Daniel Hawkins. If you do, I want you to listen close, because in my own mind I know Daniel killed Jerry Sykes. Until today I didn't have enough to make a case against him. But now I could bring him to trial and build up a circumstantial case against him that would send him to jail for the rest of his life, maybe worse. Why? Because he ran away and juries aren't apt to believe a man who has to be brought back in handcuffs."

Clem began to walk slowly back and forth in the room. Gilly's eyes did not follow him, but remained fixed on a point directly in front of her. "But I don't want to have to do it that way. Not because I want to favor Daniel but because I don't want him punished beyond what's right. I know Daniel and I knew Jerry. Everybody that was at the dance says Jerry was drunk that night and quarrelsome. What could have happened if he'd run into Daniel outside somewheres—a boy he'd been deviling ever since they were school kids, a boy who'd been hurt for a long time and kept it quiet and locked up inside himself not knowing it was festering into hate? What would have happened if Jerry picked a fight with Daniel, and suddenly all of Daniel's hate broke out and before he knew it, he'd killed a man?"

"Is that the way you think it happened?" Gilly asked, her voice sad and somehow distant, almost as if she were alone in the room and asking the question of herself.

The sheriff shrugged his shoulders heavily. "I don't know. You can't figure this the way you would a game of checkers. All I know is that it sounds reasonable. But only Daniel Hawkins can tell us what happened. That's the reason I want him to come back of his own accord, so a jury will believe what he says. Because if he speaks the truth freely I think the truth will help him."

He looked at the girl. She was sitting rigidly still, staring straight ahead of her as if she hadn't been listening.

"What are you thinking, girl?"

Her gray eyes didn't shift and when she spoke it was to herself again. "He was so troubled always—"

The sheriff looked down at her gently. "You knew it all the time, didn't you, knew it and tried not to believe it."

"No!" The word came out with such violence that the sheriff was startled. "No—never. Never. Never!"

The sheriff waited uncomfortably, hoping that the girl would not burst into tears. But when she raised her head again there was no sign of weeping, and her face was as cold and impassive as marble.

"You needn't stay any longer, Miss Johnson," the sheriff said. "Only if you know where you can find the boy, find him. If you can talk to him, tell him to come back, before it's too late, while there's still time for him to pay his punishment and have most of his life left to live like an ordinary human being."

The sheriff did not hear an answer as he stood behind his desk. All he heard was the slow sound of her footsteps as she crossed the room, opened the door, and went out.

Clem was still standing there when George came into the office. "Get anywhere with the girl?" George asked.

Clem shrugged his shoulders. He pulled out the desk drawer, took out a handful of badges, and tossed them on top of the papers littering the desk. "Fetch me some deputies," he said.

There were the magnolias, their blossoms long-rotted in the autumn earth, the great cloud of branches that hung about the brick and flaked white woodwork, the cornices and shuttered windows and gaping roof of Blackwater mansion. Outside was the night without a moon, the night in which there were only shades of blackness. But within the deeper darkness of the room the outer shadow penetrated here and there as if it were light. He had stumbled when he first came into the room and a thin-legged chair had rattled noisily as he fell against it. But now he was able to see things—the chair stuffing pulled out by rats, the dim marble of the corner fireplace with the mantel clock unwound for a third of a century, the ancient canopy of the bed, its folds coated with years of dust. He wiped his hand across a framed engraving. Beneath his hand stood Lee on the field at Antietam—a man alone, fighting a cause now as lost and dead as everything else in this room.

And yet, in the stale and motionless air, there still hung a thin, musty fragrance, like dried flowers in a book, a fragrance that told of other evenings in which some kind of life had invaded this lifeless room—of him and Gilly listening to the storm beating against the shutters, of the night they had gone through the house from top to bottom, and in the stray moonlight in the ballroom, with its silent piano and rickety chairs along the walls, Gilly had half turned in an old waltz step as if music were playing. That was make-believe, and the make-believe was over. Blackwater mansion had seemed like a sanctuary. It was only a dirty prison—a prison from which he could escape only by leaving everything behind.

Mose too. A few minutes ago he had watched Mose's lantern swinging as the black man returned from the dog kennel to his shanty. Now, as Danny looked down through the lattices of the shutter toward the dim glow of Mose's window, he heard a few distant chords and runs on the guitar and suddenly wished that he could go down and sit on the step as he had always done. But that was over too—he couldn't even say goodbye, tell Mose that in a little while he was leaving Blackwater behind him forever. He and Mose were separated now, separated as if they were strangers.

Somewhere in the house a bit of plaster struck the floor as a rat ran through the wall. Then a board creaked—or was it a branch scraping the roof? Danny stood dead quiet, listening. He'd better start moving, he thought. He'd already waited an hour longer than was necessary after dark, and there was no telling what was happening right now in town, at the sheriff's office, at Aunt Jessie's. Suddenly he turned tensely. The board had creaked again—only it wasn't the same board.

In the gloom of the doorway stood Gilly.

In silence they faced each other across the darkened room. Then he heard her uncertain voice. "Danny?"

He took a step toward her and when he spoke his voice had suddenly become bitter and harsh. "What are you doing here?"

"You didn't say goodbye."

"I didn't have time."

"And you weren't coming back—ever?" The words seemed small,

pinched.

"No."

"Then you are running away?"

"If you want to call it that."

"Why?" The question hung there in the dark, unanswered, while Danny tried to understand why she had asked it.

"Don't you know?" he asked bitterly. "I thought the sheriff would have his deputies running all over the county by now."

"He has," her voice, even again, answered him.

"Then why'd you come here?" he repeated, his voice suddenly loud, not with anger but with a pleading desperation. "To help him? To show him where I was?"

"No," she said quietly. "To ask."

"Don't ask what you know already."

"Always you were trying to tell me something," she said, still motionless, still distant. "Tell me now."

"You want me to say I killed a man," he said. He looked at her for a long moment before he went on heavily. "All right. I'll say it. I killed Jerry Sykes. I killed him with a rock—the guy you were going to marry—the night I took you off the floor at Brothers Landing. He asked for it, like he'd been asking for it ever since we were kids."

Danny paused. It seemed as if there was a great gash in his body where his lungs were, as if the air he was taking into his body wasn't really air, but something dead and stifling, and yet his heart pounded fast and painfully as if it had expanded and was bursting against his ribs, each beat an explosion. "I was glad then, because I hated him," Danny said as he tried to breathe. "And I thought I done right. But I ain't glad no more. I didn't know, when I killed him, that I was doing a thing to please him most, that now he could really hound me, till they caught me—like coon in a tree. Only I ain't going to let it happen—not like coon. Ain't nobody going to shake me out of a tree."

Across the room a voice, soft and distant, asked him, "Why didn't you tell me before?"

"I tried but I didn't dare," Danny said tiredly. "I tried every time I saw you, every time you talked about Jerry. I wanted to tell you you were blind, that the man who'd killed Jerry was standing beside you, talking to you, holding your hand. But I couldn't—"

"I wouldn't have gone to the sheriff."

"That wasn't what stopped me," he said. "I was afraid of losing you. I was afraid you'd hate me forever." Danny lifted his head heavily and faced her across the darkness. "But I'm not afraid anymore—not of anybody, not of you. I ain't got anything to lose anymore, so why should I be afraid?"

He walked slowly back to the window and looked down toward Mose's shack, but he hardly heard the music. Suddenly he wheeled. "Why don't you go?"

For a moment there was no answer and he repeated with anger, "Why don't you go?"

And at last the small voice answered, "Where?"

"Bradford—Miss Simpkins'—your home town—anyplace."

"No," she said.

He watched her move toward him, at last saw the dim ghost become hair and face and eyes. She stood there before him, her shoulders somehow smaller and tighter under her coat. "I was afraid before," she said slowly, "because I felt something terrible between us, but it wasn't real. Now it's real and I'm not afraid."

Danny looked past her blond head, past her eyes, holding himself rigid. "It's over," he said tightly. "It was over before we even began, that first night at the dance. We were dancing, but we were already dead—like Jerry where I left him in the water."

"Over between us?"

"How can you stay with a man that did a killing? It ain't natural."

"You don't always love people for what they do. You love them for what they are—or what they need."

"I don't need anybody."

"You need more than anybody I've ever known." She hesitated. "More even than me."

He looked down at her, met her eyes in the shadow. For the first time there was gentleness in his voice. "Don't you understand?" he pleaded. "Can't you understand? What we had is over—we never had a right to it. I started something and now I got to finish it. What happens from here on is all bad and you can't have any part of it. I'm in it alone—"

"Then you should have sent me away long ago—when I might have gone. It's too late now."

"Why?"

"Because I am a part of it," she said quietly. "As long as I live."

"Gilly—" he began, then stopped. In the darkness her eyes caught his, held them.

"And now don't hurt me anymore," she said gently. "Please, Daniel—put your arms around me."

He drew her toward him.

He lay there on the rotted counterpane, his head on her lap as he stared at the ceiling, thinking: Pretty soon I must start traveling, pretty soon I must say goodbye. Every minute that passed was a more dangerous minute. There would be men on the roads, at intersections, search parties. Before morning every farmer in Bradford County would know he was a fugitive. And yet, as he thought of flight, he felt the touch of her hand softly brushing against his forehead, the warm light fingers that held him where he was, minute after minute. If she had not come it would have been easier—he would not have forgotten the pain that came to him each time he thought of her, but he could have carried it. It was different from saying goodbye, different from the terrible minute when you still tried to hold on to what you had, and the soft gentle fingers were telling you that maybe you could. Only the fingers were wrong. You couldn't.

He turned his eyes toward her white face bent above him, watching him as her hand touched his forehead. Her fingers still continued their slight patient movement as she said softly, "Now I can see your face."

He smiled a little in the darkness. She leaned closer toward him. "I was so afraid before—when I came. You stood across the room. I couldn't see you. It was like those other times, only worse."

"What other times?"

"When we were together but there was a hand holding you back, a secret in your eyes—a stranger who made me afraid."

"You should be more afraid now."

"No," she said. "Now I know who you are."

"Is that why you stayed?"

"A part of it, maybe—" She hesitated as she looked down at him. Suddenly she asked, "How old are you, Daniel?"

"Twenty-three. Why?"

"Sometimes your face looks so young—almost a boy's face. An unhappy boy."

A grim joke crossed his mind. "The law says I'm a man."

She was silent and it seemed to him that a sudden sharp sadness had crossed her dim face.

"What is it?" he asked.

"You can be a man," she said softly. "A fine man, a good man—the finest man I've ever known." Again she paused for an instant before she said, "Right now, you're like a little boy who's lost."

He didn't answer. It's getting late, he thought, I got to get moving. Then he heard her voice again, "Daniel—"

"Yes?"

"You've got to go back."

Again the weary confusion in his skull. "I told you before," he said. "Not yet. Maybe someday—"

"Someday might not be soon enough."

"I ain't clear, I got to get answers."

"Maybe you won't find the answers this way—not for the rest of your life."

"Maybe."

He felt the silence harden as she withdrew her hand. How can I explain to her, he thought—how can I explain when I can't even explain to myself? How can I tell her it's more than being scared, that it's things you got to know in your mind like what's right and what's wrong before you give yourself to the sheriff. Else you're no better than coon—caught in a tree and not knowing how or why it all happened.

"Where will you go?" she asked finally, her voice sad and far away once more.

"I don't know," he said, trying to think about it. "Maybe Chinamook, maybe to Grandma's—but not for long." He stopped and then added as if it were something he had thought of many times before, "Pa and Ma are buried together on top the ridge back of Grandma's place."

"You never knew them?"

"No."

"And after that," she asked, "where will you go?"

"I don't know."

She watched him silently, her face an indistinct mask above him. It was as if life had gone out of it, and all that was left was the tiredness of the dead. "What are you thinking?" he asked.

She shrugged tiredly. "Only what it will be like tomorrow. Going into the classroom—the chalk and the children's feet shuffling and the bell ringing for the period. I'll ask questions about a lot of dead history—the names of the thirteen colonies and what year Jamestown was settled. And you—and you?"

She twisted her head aside suddenly and Danny felt her body grow rigid and tremble. He raised himself slightly and seized her hand, but it lay loose and cold in his. "Gilly," he said. "Gilly, we're dreaming—we're only hurting ourselves!"

"I know," she whispered, and then as he tried to seize her, she shook away his hand. "Please go—if you must!"

"Maybe someday—" He put his hand on her arm and held it rigid while his eyes remained fixed on a point in the ceiling above them.

It was dark now. But for just a moment a flashlight beam had shot up through the gaps in the lattice, swung briefly across the ceiling and upper wall, and disappeared.

"Listen!" he whispered.

Gilly sat upright in the dark, speechless, as Danny moved silently from the bed toward the shuttered window. Through the lattices he could see a small group of five or six men, hear their indistinct voices as they argued whether or not it was worth searching the old mansion.

"What'd be the sense of his coming here?" Danny recognized the deputy sheriff's voice. "Once he got started he'd keep moving."

Another voice, one that Danny didn't recognize, asked, "Suppose the black man was telling the truth that he hadn't seen him? The boy was out here a lot."

Once more the flashlight played across the side of the house. "Don't see no windows been pried," said Ed, the deputy. Then their voices were lost as the group moved around a corner of the mansion.

Danny moved back across the room toward Gilly. She got up and faced him. "I'm going, Gilly. Ain't no more time. Maybe it's too late now. But I'm going to try. I want you to stay till I'm gone."

"Yes."

He looked into her face, held her gaze steady for an instant, then reached out his hand and touched her face. "Goodbye, Gilly Johnson!"

She did not answer.

She was still standing in the silent room, no longer hearing him anywhere, when the voices of the men sounded excitedly from the front portico. Almost at once she heard a rattling at the great front door, a rattling that echoed through the barren house. Slowly she began moving toward the head of the hall stairs and started down just as the door burst open so suddenly that three men nearly sprawled into the lower hallway.

"She was open all the time!" a man cried out, and a flashlight beam swung across the hall and up the stairs toward Gilly. It passed her and came back, its blinding light in her eyes.

For half a second there was only the hush in which one man muttered, "I told you it was a lady's footprint." And then Clem Otis's tired voice called out, "Come on down, Gilly Johnson!"

He waited until the girl had crossed from the last step toward the door before he asked, "Where's Daniel?"

"He isn't here." Her voice was calm, almost uninterested.

"How long's he been gone?"

"I won't say."

"You're aiding and abetting a criminal."

"I know."

The sheriff's eyes searched her quiet face grimly. He turned. "George, you and one of the boys look over the house. Then come down to Mose's shack right away. I'm going to fetch the dogs."

He spoke to Gilly again. "You better come down to the shack with me."

The sheriff already had four of the dogs on leashes when George and his partner came down from the mansion to say that the house was empty. "All right, George," Clem said. "We'll take the dogs up there and cast for the trail." He looked at the Negro, standing straight and tall and silent in the grassy lane. "You ready, Mose?"

"You're not going to ask me to go hunting for my friend, are you, Sheriff?" Mose said without moving.

"I need you to handle the dogs," Clem said.

"I wish they was dead," Mose said simply.

Gilly moved to the sheriff. "Let me come," she said quietly.

"You?" said Clem, surprised. "How's a woman going to keep up with the dogs?"

"I'll follow. I'll not worry you."

Clem looked at her for a moment, then handed the leashes to George. "I don't recommend it," he said. "But you can take your own chances. Come on, George. We're losing time."

In the darkness Danny was running wildly along the path that led away from the spring house. He felt light, as though his legs and body had ceased to exist, and he was hardly conscious of his feet as they beat down on the uneven path. In the gloom of the clouded night he could not see more than a few steps ahead, and yet he never stumbled, never fell.

Abruptly the path ended. Danny found himself in a thicket of long-forgotten berry bushes that clung to his clothes and slashed his arms with thorns as sharp as razors. He pushed them back savagely with his hands, not feeling the thorns in his flesh. Beyond the brambles a barrier of alders struck him like sticks, then at last he was at the edge of a stump-strewn field.

From the moment that he had dropped to the ground from the second-story window and crept to the shadow of the spring house

Danny had known that his only safety lay in the swamp—and even there for no more than the few hours it would take the sheriff to circle the swamp and pick up Danny's trail again where he emerged to higher ground. Danny didn't know whether the sheriff had decided to search Blackwater mansion or if they'd found Gilly. All he knew was that if they had, time was short. It wouldn't take the dogs long to find his trail.

He started across the field diagonally to reach the far side where he could take his bearing before moving into the swamp, but his feet were less certain now and his body less light. The ground had become a dark uneven thing in which each step held a trap, a furrow or a mound that would jar his body and throw him awkwardly to the side. Beyond him the black wall of trees that hemmed the field was drawing closer.

Then suddenly, as he reached the far corner, the field turned at right angles into another clearing and there, close by, stood a tobacco barn with white wood smoke curling up from its chimney pipe. Under the little porch at one end a Negro stoker lay before the grate of the oven on a couch of burlap bags. Danny saw him get up on one elbow and raise his lantern as he peered into the darkness. At last the Negro lowered his lantern and lay back on the couch again.

Danny circled the tobacco barn slowly until he reached the far edge of the clearing, and there under the trees he threw himself onto the ground. As far as he could make out he had come a little over a mile. The edge of Blackwater swamp lay a half mile deeper in the woods where the tree-grown bog reached out and spread over the low ground toward Brothers Pond. If the dogs came he would still have time to reach the swamp and lose them in the brackish shallows.

But he had hardly fallen to the ground before he got to his feet again. Back at Blackwater mansion the dogs had found his trail. He could hear their yelping, distinct and clear, cutting across the silent night.

Again he ran but now it seemed as if his body had doubled its weight, as if it were some great load holding him back, making his feet stagger over tree roots and rocks. And yet he felt no pain—only the increasing heaviness of his body moving forward drunkenly on his powerless legs. It was hard to tell where the dogs were because an uncertain wind kept veering, sometimes holding back the sound and then suddenly bringing it immeasurably closer.

When at last his feet sank into the bog, and the dark growth of tree and root and rotted log closed around him, Danny felt a desperate desire to drop where he was, but he knew that he was not yet safe, that he must go deeper into the swamp. He stumbled forward, feeling the wet ground sink beneath him, the cold water seep into his shoes, and the icy backwaters chill his kneecaps as he waded, thigh-deep, through the white low-lying layer of fog.

He climbed onto a fallen tree trunk, reached his hand into the slime and coated his face with it before he stretched out. Then he waited. In his mind he tried to follow the dogs by their baying. Now they had reached the clearing where the old Negro was, now they were among the trees, now they had reached the swamp. There the baying became scattered, falling away to an intermittent yelp as the dogs crashed futilely through the brush or splashed through the shallows in search of the scent. Once, lying on the log, Danny heard the men's voices very distinctly as they called back the dogs.

For a long time after the swamp had become silent again, Danny lay on the log. He began to tremble—the cold was numbing his wet legs. Slowly he raised himself from the log, felt his legs sink downward again through the knee-deep water. Once more he moved forward, trying to make no splash or sound which would echo in the tomb-like silence. If he was lucky, if he kept his bearing, he would reach high ground within two hours.

Chapter Nine

It was night again when Danny sat at the long table in his grandmother's cabin and looked at the rough-slabbed walls, the ash-powdered hearth, the Winchester above the mantel, thinking: This is my home, this is where I was born, this is what I remember. Nothing had changed—not the worn table nor the tin dipper hanging on the peg above the bucket, nor the wooden crib in which he had been rocked, nor the forest and sky beyond the window, nor the silence of the mountain night. He had not heard the dogs since they had turned back from Blackwater swamp.

Across the table the old woman stretched out her hand and turned the wick in the lamp upward to increase the light. Then she bent over the cigar box again and Danny could hear her gnarled fingers rustling clumsily through the papers in it. He looked at her. She had not changed either. In his memory she had seemed no less old when he was a child, her face no less furrowed, her mouth no less pinched with age. The black shawl she wore about her gray hair was still the shawl that she had worn fifteen years ago. Only now as he watched her could he notice that her body seemed less erect and sure, and that her head nodded persistently as if it were too heavy for her frail neck.

She removed a packet of broken yellow newsprint, tied with a string, and laid them on the table. "No," he said, "not those."

They were the clippings of his father's trial.

She lifted a single bit of torn newspaper from the box and held it across the table. Danny took it carefully as he heard his grandmother's dimmed voice say, "Jeb never had a picture took in his life—not till the trial."

Danny looked at it. The clipping was faded now, so faded that the features of his father's face were hardly visible. All that remained were the great shock of black hair, the sharp contours of the jaw, the eyes that looked straight out from beneath the broad forehead.

It was a mountaineer's face, the face of a man who'd never bent in his life. This was the face that Danny had met more than once in his dreams—grim, hunted, and condemned.

"Your Aunt Jessie sent them up from the local papers," said his grandmother, her head nodding gently as she spoke. She took the clipping from where Danny had put it down. "You're your father's son, Daniel." Her eyes, still sharp and alive, flickered toward him. "Especially the eyes and the voice."

"What kind of voice?" Danny asked.

"Low, but not weak," she answered. "Funny thing. Jeb Hawkins never raised his voice—'less he was happy. Then you could hear him across mountains."

Danny stared across the table at the old woman as a shock passed through him. "What's that about Pa?" he asked.

His grandmother looked at him vaguely as if she hadn't understood. "About his voice?"

"About Pa being happy," he said, a sudden tension in his voice. "When was Pa happy?"

"Jeb?" she asked. "Why, he could kick the floor louder than eight horses when there was a good fiddler at the dance. A prime man, Jeb was, a prime man. When my Betty married him wasn't anybody between Chinamook and Bradford to match him for singing." Grandma's eyes suddenly seemed to stop seeing Danny. It was as if they were seeing something else instead, in her mind, a long time ago. "Never forget the night they come back from the wedding—back to this cabin Jeb had built special with his own hands. It was sunup and they been dancing all the time, but when they come in the door there your pa looked like he'd never need to sleep again in his life. That fresh he was—still full of sparks as a fresh log." Grandma's voice dimmed away as if she was only repeating something her mind was saying. "Kind of gentled off, though, after he got married. You were the only young one, and you were a long time coming."

Danny got up slowly and walked across the floor toward the window. A night wind had begun to blow up the dark valley, tossing the tops of the pines silhouetted against the sky. Never in my life I been happy, thought Daniel—never. Wasn't no girls watching me at the dance unless they was thinking I was the son of a criminal. Wasn't nobody wanted to give me a job even, till they was shorthanded on the railroad. Wasn't nobody ever made me happy enough to sing—except Gilly, and that's too late. There ain't going to be no wedding for me, no wedding to dance at till five in the morning, no house to bring her home to afterward. Nothing.

Danny struggled to fight back the resentment rising in him. All his life he had thought of his father as a man persecuted and unsmiling—a man who had only suffered, then finally rebelled and lost. Every beating, every lonely hour, every sly insult half heard behind his back Danny had accepted for his father, in defense of his father, and when he'd killed Jerry—was that for his father too? But he knew all the while what he was doing—he was defending his father and his father's name. He was fighting against the wrong they did him, and even though Jeb Hawkins was dead on the gallows, Danny had still felt that he was a partner—a silent partner no longer able to defend himself.

But now suddenly something terrible had changed. Danny had been loyal to a man that never existed, a ghost he had only imagined in his mind. Somehow, and in a way that he could only partly understand, this new father who walked in his grandmother's mind had betrayed him, and all the aching, resentful years of his life were for no cause that mattered. This new father had lived like any ordinary man—happy, like Grandma said—and his shooting of the doctor was a futile rage to revenge a wife already dead. He had paid for his rage in three weeks' time—and Danny, Danny had carried the weight of his father's guilt for all the twenty-three years of his life.

Behind him he heard his grandmother say quietly, "He was mighty proud of you, Daniel."

Danny wheeled abruptly from the window and the night outside. "Well, I ain't proud of Pa," he said full of slow and painful anger. "Never no more I'm not!"

"Can't hold something against a dead man, Daniel," she answered without turning to look at him. "Some folks say he done wrong, some say he done right. I say Jeb acted like the man he was, settling a question quick and hard. But he loved Betty—and he loved you."

"He damned me!" The words wrenched out of Danny's mouth— words he could not stop. "He damned me all my life for what he did! Maybe you can't hold something against a dead man like you say, but he held what he did against me ever since I was born. Ain't been a day when I haven't heard of it or felt it and wanted a different name from what I had. Before he killed the doctor why didn't he think of the living instead of the dead?"

"Jeb did—after it was too late," Grandma said slowly. "But he thought of it all the same. He could have gone over the ridge and down to the big river, gone down the river on a log at night—but he didn't. He could have killed a couple of the sheriff's men when they come across the clearing to get him—but he didn't do that either. He waited almost where you're standing right now. 'I think I done right,' he told me. 'But if I done wrong like they say, I'm going to square it. Then maybe they'll forget—and leave the boy be, not make him grow up paying for what I done.'"

Grandma sat in the chair, her hands folded in her lap just like Aunt Jessie. "Took a man to say that, Daniel," she said gently. "It's only a coward that blames what he does on everybody else."

Danny looked at his grandmother while her words slowly felt their way into his baffled mind. "Even when it ain't his fault?" he asked.

"Even then," she said. Grandma was silent again before she said, "You ain't got a right to hate your pa, Daniel. He did his best to protect you from suffering for what he did. Told me to send you away, give you another name. I sent you away, but I didn't change your name. That was my doing. I was proud of that name."

Danny did not answer. He stood there, torn by a confusing storm that beat at him from all sides. He was looking for answers but they didn't come easy—or maybe they came too easy and too many. For every question there were at least two answers—maybe a hundred. Maybe Gilly was right. Maybe he'd look for the rest of his life and never know, never really know. And yet how could you live without knowing—or at least making up your mind. The one definite thing he'd always stood by wasn't true—it was a lie. He was losing his father, watching him die in his mind, an unreal destroyed image—and now a stranger was standing beside him saying, "I'm your father."

Then, still standing, he began to listen, listen to a familiar sound carried up the valley toward him on the wind. He looked quickly at his grandmother, but her head remained bent over the cigar box as she carefully returned the papers to it. For an eternity he watched her stiff hands patiently stack the papers neatly in the box. At last she closed it and got up.

She stood there gazing at him through her old eyes. "I know now why you want to hate your pa," she said. "I wondered what brought you back after so long—your hands bleeding and the mud on you."

"Leave me be, Grandma."

"Your pa could have gone over the ridge and down the big river," she said, still watching him. "You could too. Won't no dogs follow you there."

"You telling me to run away?"

"No," she said. "Only a man has to handle himself in his own way. Good night to you, Daniel."

He watched her move past him, her head gently nodding as she walked slowly across the floor and into the small room where she kept her bed.

"Good night, Grandma," he murmured after she could no longer hear.

For a long while after he had blown out the flame in the lamp Danny sat on the old chest by the window listening to the wind and watching the night clouds run past a young, cold moon. For a time he had heard intermittently the baying of the dogs, but now the baying had ceased once more and there was only the sound of the wind shaking the pines. They've bedded down, Danny thought—they've lost the trail where I went into the creek and they won't find it again till morning. I still got four, maybe five hours to sleep before I go over the ridge and down to the big river like Grandma said.

He went across the room and took down the Winchester, found the cartridges in the tea can on the mantel and slid one into the breech. Then he went back again to the chest and leaned back against the window sill, the gun cradled in his arms. The last embers in the fireplace were hidden in ash and the room with all its familiar things lay around him in the dim darkness. And yet somehow Danny sensed uneasily that the room was no longer familiar, that he no longer belonged to it or it to him. He had been born here, lived in this room for the first ten years of his life, and yet now it was suddenly secret and strange to him—as if something alive had died here and he were sitting at its wake. But nothing had changed. The table was the same table, the crib the same crib, the walls the same walls. Maybe it's just me that's changed, in ways I don't know or understand.

I got to sleep, he thought, I got to sleep. I ain't had more than six hours out of forty-eight and my legs feel like they was doped—ain't going to carry me much farther if I don't sleep. Maybe if I closed my eyes I'd stop thinking, stop going round in circles, stop trying to make odd numbers come out even. Maybe I'd wake up and my head would be clear again and things would be simple.

But it wasn't any good closing his eyes. His head was full of words all talking at once, and all talking in different voices—voices like Gilly or Mose or Aunt Jessie or Grandma. They were all trying to help him, all giving him answers. But they weren't helping him, they were just mixing him up, and he felt the way he had in the black swamp, running into trees and stumbling over roots, praying that he'd kept his bearing, praying that he'd get to high ground before his legs collapsed under him.

Or was he just kidding himself when he said he wanted to find the answers? Maybe it was the last thing he wanted to find; maybe that was why he was trying to run away from the words in his mind, trying not to listen. What was it Grandma had said? Something about it was only a coward who tried to blame what he did on everybody else? Well, maybe she was right, maybe that was what he was doing. He'd blamed the town, he'd blamed Jerry, he'd blamed even his father for the killing—but he wasn't taking his share of the fault, the biggest share. What he'd done to Jerry was worse than anything anybody had ever done to him in his life, and yet he was trying to throw off the blame. His father had done better—he did a wrong thing but believed it was right and still paid off to try to protect Danny.

Maybe that was what Grandma was driving at when she said you had to pay off even when your wrong wasn't all your fault. Bradford could be wrong, Jerry could be wrong—but it still didn't make right what he'd done. You had to take responsibility and pay your share of the check—or else who paid it? And suddenly he knew—your friends paid it. They paid it and forgave you and you didn't even say thanks. Or maybe you couldn't just say thanks. You had to pay off for their sake as well as your own.

Mose had said that killing wasn't simple, that when you killed a man you also killed the part that belonged to anybody who ever knew him. Maybe there was more to it, maybe when you did something as terrible as killing it wasn't just you that carried the guilt but you made anyone that loved you carry it too. Like the sailor with the albatross around his neck—he hadn't just cursed himself. He'd cursed every other man on his ship. All my life, Danny thought, I been looking for a friend, somebody to talk to—nothing else. And when I found them I made them carry my hate. I nearly killed Billy for it, I let Mose's guitar do his crying for him, I left a hurt in Gilly's eyes that'll stay there long as she lives. Can't nobody take it away except me, except me going back.

That ain't the whole answer, Danny thought, but maybe it's a part of it. At least I got a bearing and maybe it'll take me to the high ground. Maybe I can think better when I'm not so tired. Maybe tomorrow. Tomorrow he could go down the big river like Grandma said, float downstream for miles in a night on a log. He could get to Memphis, New Orleans, Mexico maybe. The world was a big place, a man could get lost easy in it. But was it big enough?

All my life, Danny thought, I'm going to be a stranger. All my life I'm going to see Gilly's face when I said goodbye at Blackwater mansion. All my life I'm going to hear them dogs in the back of my head. All my life I ain't going to have no company except the man I killed.

Outside the wind was rising. I got to sleep, he told himself. I got to sleep.

And very quietly he began to cry.

When Danny awoke it was still dark, the darkness before dawn. For a moment he lay there thinking that he was in his room at Aunt Jessie's. Then he felt the rifle lying against his arm and knew once more where he was. He raised himself to the window and looked out. The wind had died down, the moon was gone, and the valley lay silent and black between the ridges. Down there somewhere the men and dogs were still asleep.

He got up and walked stiffly to the crib full of tinder, threw some kindling in the fireplace, and carefully held a dry split log upon it. After he had set a match to it he watched the blaze climb up over the log, warming the room and filling it with shadowy movement. Then he searched the cupboard for biscuits and went back to the fire, eating them slowly as he felt the chill of the night leave his body.

When he opened the cabin door and went out to the path that led to the spring, the darkness was already thinning, and over Black Mountain a few high clouds were touched with pink. But under the trees the shadows still lay deep and a cool morning breeze rustled the leaves. As he descended the steep path Danny remembered other mornings, the mornings when he was a little boy and had always stolen carefully down the path to make as little noise as possible. He had never known what game he might find near the spring and he remembered the excitement he had felt when he had frightened a seven-point buck as it was drinking. In his mind the spring at the early morning hour had always been a place somehow secret, somehow his alone.

He lay down on the rock beside the spring, partly supporting himself on his hands, then lowered his head and felt the cold, sweet taste of the water in his mouth. He drank deeply, the water moving like a chill current down his throat into his body. As he raised himself he suddenly saw his own face reflected in the spring. Danny hesitated. He was remembering something—the washroom mirror at Roy's, the strange sensation of knowing that he had just killed a man and yet finding his face unchanged, unmarked. It was still the same face, still unchanged—no different from the one in the mirror. And yet now, for the first time, Danny knew that behind his face something had changed again.

I'm going back, he thought, as if the scales had fallen from his eyes and he had just seen a miracle. I'm going back. I'm not going over the ridge and down to the big river, I'm not going to run away no more. I'm not going to fight it out with the Winchester because you only need a Winchester when you're going to kill and I ain't going to kill no more. They can hang me on a tree, but I ain't going to kill no more.

Without pausing at the cabin he went up to the ridge to the crest where Jeb and Betty Hawkins lay under the pines with the stone markers on their graves. There were only a few leaves skittering over them as Danny stood there, no longer full of hate or anger but only a gentle sadness. I ain't proud of what you done, Pa, he thought, but all the same I didn't mean what I said last night. You did the best you could to even up and that's what I'm doing now. Then maybe both of us can have some peace.

Far down the valley a gun was fired. Once more Danny heard the baying of the dogs.

He turned, faced Black Mountain and the whole valley where he was born. He could see the rim of the sun and the shadow climbing up the side of the mountain, leaving only the thin trail of mist hanging above Chinamook creek.

He started down the slope toward the sound of the dogs. He walked lightly in great increasing steps as if in this morning he had suddenly become a giant.

Before him lay a clearing. As he started across it a single dog suddenly bounded from the shelter of the trees and sped toward him. "Here, Daisy Bell!" he called.

Daisy Bell faltered in her stride, stopped, and, lowering her belly to the ground, crawled toward him where he waited. He nipped her ear and felt her cold nose nuzzling his hand.

He was still crouched beside the dog when he heard a movement in the tall grass, saw the booted legs and gun barrels in a semicircle around him. He looked up. Clem Otis was watching him oddly.

"Hello, Sheriff," said Danny softly.

Clem stared at him. "What made you come back, son?" There was a sudden huskiness in his voice.

"I changed my mind," Danny answered.

"I thought you would—if I gave you enough time," said Clem slowly. "I was afraid I wouldn't have enough time to give."

Danny heard another small movement in the high grass beyond the sheriff—a sound he could not identify—and yet there was a knowledge in the sheriff's face that made him get up slowly, his heart pounding. Ten feet away Gilly stood motionless, waiting.

He took a step toward her. "Gilly—" he said, and found it difficult to say. "You were right—about finding the answers. I'm never going to find them anyplace—only here."

"I'm glad, Daniel, very glad," she said so softly and tiredly he could hardly hear her. Then she was close to him, and Danny, looking down at the streaked face and tousled hair, suddenly saw it blur in front of him as his eyes filled.

Behind them George stepped forward and silently opened a handcuff, began to attach it to Danny's wrist.

But Sheriff Clem Otis's head suddenly hooked forward. "Here! What you doing there?" he asked sharply. "Leave the boy be. Let him walk back—like a man."

THE END

FILM NOIR CLASSICS

THE PITFALL Jay Dratler
"Dratler's novel is darker, sleazier and less forgiving than the film it inspired. A brutal portrait of blind lust and self-destruction... a stellar example of 1940s American noir." —Cullen Gallagher, *Pulp Serenade*. Filmed in 1948 with Dick Powell, Lizabeth Scott, Jane Wyatt and Raymond Burr.

FALLEN ANGEL Marty Holland
"This story, about a small-time grifter who lands in a central California town and hooks up with a femme fatale, is straight out of the James M. Cain playbook."—Bill Ott, *Booklist*. Filmed in 1945 with Dana Andrews, Alice Faye and Linda Darnell.

**THE VELVET FLEECE
Lois Eby & John C. Fleming**
"We guarantee your head will be spinning with double-crosses and you'll be talking out of both sides of your mouth before you finish...."
—*Evening Star*. Filmed as *Larceny* in 1948 starring John Payne, Joan Caulfield and Dan Duryea.

SUDDEN FEAR Edna Sherry
"This is a thoroughly exciting read, with brilliant pacing, which makes you absolutely desperate to know how everything will pan out."
—Kate Jackson. Filmed in 1952 with Joan Crawford, Jack Palance and Gloria Grahame.

HOLLOW TRIUMPH Murray Forbes
"...a disturbed personality done in the noir tradition... an atmospheric and evocative yarn that spans the late 30s to through WWII."—Amazon reader. Filmed in 1948 with Paul Henreid and Joan Bennett as *The Scar*.

**THE DARK CORNER /
SLEEP, MY LOVE Leo Rosten**
"The slang is tangy, the plots magnetic, the suspense sweet, the hilarity edgy... For all lovers of vintage noir."
—Donna Seaman, *Booklist*. Filmed in 1946 and 1948 with Lucille Ball, Clifton Well, Claudette Colbert and Robert Cummings.

**DEADLIER THAN THE MALE
James Gunn**
"The attitude of the book... reels between black comedy and surrealism drenched in a misanthropy that is occasionally stunning."—Ed Gorman. Filmed as *Born to Kill* in 1947 with Lawrence Tierney and Claire Trevor.

**KISS THE BLOOD OFF MY HANDS
Gerald Butler**
"The violence, crime, brutality, and 'trapped-in-a-narrow-place' aspects of noir are all here."—Carl Waluconis. Filmed in 1948 with Joan Fontaine and Burt Lancaster.

In trade paperback from...
Stark House Press, 1315 H Street, Eureka, CA 95501
greg@starkhousepress.com / www.StarkHousePress.com
Available from your local bookstore, or order direct via our website.

Made in the USA
Monee, IL
15 October 2024

68008667R00089